GRIFFIN
The Mavericks, Book 02

Dale Mayer

GRIFFIN: THE MAVERICKS, BOOK 2
Beverly Dale Mayer
Valley Publishing Ltd.

ISBN-13: 978-1-773362-01-4
Print Edition

About This Book

What happens when the very men—trained to make the hard decisions—come up against the rules and regulations that hold them back from doing what needs to be done? They either stay and work within the constraints given to them or they walk away. Only now, for a select few, they have another option:

The Mavericks. A covert black ops team that steps up and break all the rules … but gets the job done.

Welcome to a new military romance series by *USA Today* best-selling author Dale Mayer. A series where you meet new friends in this raw and compelling look at the men who keep us safe every day from the darkness where they operate—and live—in the shadows … until someone special helps them step into the light.

Helping Kerrick was one thing, getting tagged for a mission of his own quite another …

His heart ached to hear a young girl had been kidnapped while at a hotel in Thailand, waiting for her father to arrive. But nothing is ever as it seems, and this case isn't even close to simple.

Lorelai spent the last seven years enjoying her young charge, Amelia Rose. Tutoring the daughter of a wealthy business owner added perks to the job, like holidays around the world. In all these years Lorelai had never once seen the downside to having big money–until the holiday in Thailand where Amelia Rose is targeted, and they were both kidnapped.

Griffin managed to rescue the kidnapped victims, but tracing the kidnappers was a whole different story and brought the group a little too close to home …

Sign up to be notified of all Dale's releases here!
https://geni.us/DaleNews

Books in This Series

Kerrick, Book 1

Griffin, Book 2

Jax, Book 3

Beau, Book 4

Asher, Book 5

Ryker, Book 6

Miles, Book 7

Nico, Book 8

Keane, Book 9

Lennox, Book 10

Gavin, Book 11

Shane, Book 12

Diesel, Book 13

Jerricho, Book 14

Killian, Book 15

Hatch, Book 16

Corbin, Book 17

Aiden, Book 18

Boxed Sets and Bundles

https://geni.us/Bundlepage

CHAPTER 1

GRIFFIN TOMAS WOKE to an odd buzzing on his night table. He glanced at the clock—2:03 a.m.—then around at his surroundings. Still in the same hotel room stateside that he had been living out of for the last week. Like Kerrick, Griffin was at a crossroads. He needed a real home but had no idea where it should be. If he continued to work with the Mavericks, he could live any damn place. They'd fly him to his op. He had some ideas but …

His phone's insistent buzz brought him to full awareness. He grabbed it and frowned. "What?"

"Your services are needed," said the stoic voice on the other end.

"Again? So soon?"

"What can I say? The world's a mess," the voice said.

"Not sure if I want to do any more of these specialized jobs," he said quietly.

"Understood, but you have a unique skill set."

"And what's that?"

The other end went quiet.

Griffin wiped the sleep from his eyes. "Am I going in alone?"

"You can choose one. You'll have all the support you need in the background as usual. And, if you need more backup, you only have to ask."

"What about Kerrick?"

The voice hesitated. "How about Asher or Jax?"

"Jax? Jax Darrum?"

"Yes."

"I didn't realize he was part of the team."

"We're considering it."

Griffin laughed. "Meaning, he hasn't said yes, and you're hoping that, if you can get me to work a job with him, it'll be a yes."

"Potentially." That voice held a dry sense of humor. "Kerrick is around, so he'll run communications on this one."

"You mean, that mysterious chat window?"

A slightly muffled cough could have easily been a chuckle when the voice said, "And maybe a little more."

Griffin frowned. "What's the job?"

"You're heading out in the USS *Anzio.*"

"Wait," Griffin said. "I'm not going anywhere until I hear what the job is."

A loud sigh traveled between the phones. "The daughter of a US newspaper mogul with a home base in London has been kidnapped in Thailand and is being held there. The father has got pull in high places and is dealing with us and MI6."

"And what's stopping the military from going in and grabbing her?"

"We only have one garbled message, saying that she's married now and that she belongs with them."

"And what does she say?" he asked, frowning. "Since when did a marriage keep somebody prisoner?"

"In many countries, it does keep them a prisoner, which is why she couldn't get the word out to us that she's being held."

"How long has she been detained?"

"Three days."

At that, Griffin straightened up in bed and threw off his blanket. "Three days? And you knew about it all this time?"

"No, we only got intel that this was a possible kidnapping at midnight. We've been waiting to get confirmation."

"Well, I have to get there fast then," he said. "That's not any two-hour trip."

"True," the voice said. "We can fly you partway, but we don't want you entering the country using any of the normal methods. You're too well-known."

He swore. "So my face isn't to be anywhere?"

"No, hence the ship entering and leaving any country."

"Sure, but going from California to Southeast Asia? That's hardly a twenty-four-hour event."

"True enough. But, as you'll see, we have multiple methods. Be by the docks at 0600 sharp."

And, just like that, the voice rang off. Swearing silently, Griffin had less than four hours. He got up, quickly packed, then showered and dressed. He would need food, depending on what was going on with his transportation. He stared at the Chinese food he'd had last night and shrugged. "Cold Chinese food. Yum. I've had worse." He used food as sustenance and an energy source, hence keeping a selection of protein bars in his ready bag.

But still it wouldn't be enough. Depending on what was happening on board ship—and whether he was there officially or secretly—he might or might not be fed. He quickly finished off the chow mein, tossed the empty containers, and exited his hotel room.

He had called for a cab, but instead a black military-issued vehicle pulled up. He stepped into the passenger side and looked at the driver, surprised to see Jax. "Wow," Griffin said. "They did convince you after all. That was fast."

Jax shot him a hard look. "A one-time deal," he said. "And only because I know you're the one going out on this op."

"Not alone if you're coming with me," Griffin said, returning his friend's hard look with one of his own. He knew Jax from several overseas missions. He was a good man to have in your corner but an even better one if it entailed night work. "Apparently we're supposed to get in and out without anyone knowing we were there."

Jax shrugged his shoulders. "So what else is new?"

They parked as close to the wharf as they could. Each picked up their duffel bags and tossed it over one shoulder. Then the two men walked to the end of the docks. A Zodiac waited for them. The pilot caught sight of them, nodded toward the back, and said, "Let's go. We're late."

Shrugging at that, both men hopped into the Zodiac, and it took off without any fanfare. By the time they reached the docked cruiser, they were led to a separate room, a small sleeping area, by one silent seaman who promptly left them there. With shades of Kerrick's mission in his mind, Griffin walked in the claustrophobic room, dumped his duffel bag, and planted his hands on his hips as he stared around. "Do you know anything more about this than I do?"

"I know Jax shit," Jax said with a grin at the play on his name.

"Well, I don't know anything either," Griffin said, his tone harsh.

Just then a single rap came at the door, and a red envelope was slid underneath. Griffin quickly opened the door, hoping to see who had delivered the letter, but nobody was in the hallway. Like this was some ghost ship. He snatched up the envelope and tore it open. *Travel instructions.*

"Interesting," he said. "We're supposed to be in Thailand by noon tomorrow. *Thailand time.*"

"So we're flying parts of it then," Jax said.

"Yeah, but I already checked. Any commercial flight takes nineteen to twenty-five hours. We better be flying Air Force One to make Thailand by then. Right off the bat, we're short like fourteen hours, just because of the time differences. Could be more like fifteen hours ahead, depending on which part of Thailand we're dealing with."

Jax groaned, then threw himself on the top bunk. "In that case, … I have time to sleep now. I didn't get much shut-eye last night."

"Who did?" Griffin muttered. Trouble was, he was hungry again. The leftover Chinese food hadn't done the job. He quickly pulled out his phone to check if he had any internet. He did, since they were still in port. He sent off a text message. **Envelope received. Travel instructions received. No damn food. No coffee.**

He put away his phone and dropped to the bottom bunk, an arm across his eyes. It was one thing to be part of a well-oiled Navy SEAL team on board a ship. They did constant training when they went out to sea. Everybody had orders; everybody had instructions, and everybody had a part to play. In this scenario though, Griffin didn't know what part he was supposed to play. That had been the same problem for Kerrick. After all those years of the disciplined navy life, Griffin found the sudden freedom in his daily routines something to adjust to. But he'd do just fine, he just needed time. Something he didn't have right now.

Helping out Kerrick had been a hell of a way to drop into this all-new Mavericks system. Griffin wasn't even sure it's what he wanted to do long-term. He'd been on the fence when he'd been tagged to help out Kerrick—who was going in alone—and, well, that wasn't Griffin's kind of a play. Nobody should go into these shitstorms without backup.

And, if some woman had been kidnapped, … well, two former SEALs would have a better chance of survival and success versus a larger team from another agency. His phone buzzed, and an encrypted file popped up with a note. His eyebrows shot up at that. He quickly followed instructions to decode it and went through the file on Amelia Rose.

"That's the daughter we're supposed to find," he said, raising his phone to flash her picture to Jax. "Except the photo's beyond dated. And chances are someone else put out the cry for help."

"Is she really being held against her will?" Jax asked. "That's one of the biggest issues here. Did she put out the cry for help, or did somebody else?"

Griffin was still going through her file when he froze, looked at the date, and swore. "I'll say it wasn't her choice," Griffin snapped, studying the data in front of him.

"And how do you know that?" Jax asked.

"She's eleven years old."

Jax peered over his top bunk at Griffin on the bottom bunk and said, "What the hell?"

Griffin nodded with a grimace. "She's just a child. It says here she was kidnapped, along with her nurse and her tutor."

"And how old's the nurse? If she's gray-haired and sixty, we're in trouble."

"The nurse is sixty-eight. So, yeah, we're in trouble. The tutor, however, is thirty-two and speaks three languages. Her name is Lorelei. Lorelei James."

"So Lorelei got the word out?" Jax asked curiously.

"Most likely," he said. "But, as usual, our intel is very skimpy."

"It seems like we go into these jobs with less and less intel each time," Jax said. He waited a moment and then said, "I heard a few details about your job with Kerrick, but it went okay, didn't it?"

Griffin groaned. "It did, but it was touch-and-go a couple times. That kid, Brandon, he was something else."

"Didn't Kerrick say something about the woman he rescued being part of the same high-IQ group?"

"Yes, she's back in her lab. The entire corporate organization has been reshuffled as she stepped up in power after all the changes. Her father had also stepped up and bought a whole pile of shares and handed over voting power to her to give her complete control of the company."

"Wow," Jax said. "Not bad for her. And I guess Kerrick is sticking around Paris."

"Yeah, and he's running communications for us this time."

"What the hell does that mean?" Jax asked.

"I think it's the Mavericks command center. Nobody is allowed to know what we do, where we're from, or what our histories are."

"So, are fake IDs in that envelope for us?"

"Maybe," he said, "but I didn't think so." He grabbed the red envelope, opened it again, and then whistled gently. "Well, there are now. They were stuck to the inside of the envelope." He quickly ripped off the tape, releasing the IDs. He handed one to Jax. "This is you, *Malcolm*."

"Whoever invented these names," Jax said, "should be

shot."

"Hey, it's way more normal than your real one," Griffin said with a laugh.

"You're one to talk," Jax said. "Who names their kid after some legendary creature in Greek mythology?"

"I think Griffins are found in many different societies back then," he said. "So, whatever. It's unusual enough, but I've always liked it."

"I like mine too. But can't say much about *Malcolm*. Malcolm Harris."

"Well, that's all right in my opinion," Griffin said, groaning. "I've been renamed as *George*. George Honeycutt."

At that, Jax chuckled. "That sounds lovely."

"It makes me sound beyond old. It's supposedly an unassuming name," he said. "At least this guy has brown hair and gray eyes. Close enough to pass for me." This time he checked the inside of the envelope more thoroughly—to the point where he ripped it open. "Okay, I don't see anything else in here. But this is a journalist's media pass, and, if you look on the back, it's got a British citizen's ID card."

"Like we look like Brits," Jax said with a scoff. "And I certainly don't have an English accent."

"I don't think you need to worry about that," he said. "I think it's a case of nobody gets to look at these close enough to double-check."

Just then another single knock came. Both men hopped up, with Jax standing behind the door. Griffin hurriedly opened the door, hoping to surprise whoever was on the other side. But, once again, he saw no one. There were, however, two large trays of covered food. He looked at it and smiled. "Well, at least my text did something."

"What? Did you text, asking for food?" Jax asked, chuckling.

"Hey, if we've got a lot of traveling to do, I want to make sure I'm fed. I cannot do anything if I don't have energy."

"Oh, I agree with you. I'm just surprised you got service so fast."

"One thing I learned from that last op with Kerrick," he said, "is that anything, *absolutely anything you want*, you just ask for it. They do their best to deliver."

"Good to know." They brought the trays inside, sat down, and stared at the covered dishes. "It's still cafeteria food though, isn't it, just under a fancy domed plate?" Jax asked.

Griffin uncovered his. "But a step above," he said. "I don't know about you, but I got steak and prawns."

Jax looked at Griffin's plate in shock and said, "Seriously?" And then he lifted the lid to his plate and said, "Look at that. I do too."

"But you don't like prawns, do you?"

"No. I'll trade you for your steak."

"Hell no," Griffin said. "I'll just eat your prawns when you're done with your steak. I know you won't eat them, so I don't have to give you anything." He gave Jax a big grin. "Good deal for me."

With that, the two men quickly polished off their meals, and then, even though it was early in the morning, they stretched out, and this time both crashed.

LORELEI JAMES SAT quietly in the corner of the room. Amelia Rose was sound asleep in her arms. Finally the little girl's tears—loaded with homesickness, loss, and grief—had dried, then had sent her crashing into a deep and restorative sleep. Lorelei, still conscious, still awake, still dealt with the terror of what these bastards had done to Nurse. Lorelei had long ago forgotten the older woman's real name as everyone called her *Nurse*. It's how she wanted it.

Why had she been killed outright? And yet, Lorelei and Amelia Rose had been also kidnapped and kept alive. In Lorelei's mind, she figured that their kidnappers had deemed Lorelei an asset whereas Nurse had been a liability. Nurse was definitely older, walked with a heavy limp, and was cantankerous and fussy, whereas Lorelei had done what they'd asked and had tried hard to be obedient. She knew in no way they would ever get out of this nightmare if she caused any more trouble. Nurse's death had been a well-heeded lesson—if that's what the kidnappers had intended.

But poor Nurse—no, Mary. That was her name. She had been with Amelia Rose since birth. And Lorelei believed Mary had been nurse to Amelia Rose's father too.

Gerard, Amelia Rose's father, would be devastated. She couldn't help but think this nightmare was due to his massive global business dealings. His media company had morphed into a worldwide media and information services company, distributing content, including book publishing, digital RE services, cable network programming, and pay-TV. Yet even though he ran his massive conglomerate from his base in England, the transplanted New Englander was, at heart, first and foremost, a family man. Nurse had sat at the dinner table with them every night.

It was very American of the entire family, but Nurse had loved it. So did Lorelei. She loved the continuity of the generations, and she loved the loyalty and affection shared between one another. Only it had suddenly shifted and not in a good way. Amelia Rose was desperately struggling to come to terms with their new reality. Lorelei could only hope the message she had managed to send off had been received. She'd taken that chance, while they were in the last hotel, with one of the cleaning ladies who had been new. Lorelei had quickly passed her the note with her plea for the cleaning lady's help, and now all Lorelei could do was wait.

At present, in their new location, no such opportunity had presented itself. Just then the door opened. She froze, the child still sleeping in her arms. One of the men came in, noted the sleeping Amelia Rose, and his face softened. That was a good-enough sign. He nodded and quickly turned and left. But then anybody who was used to dealing with children knew they were much easier to handle if they had sleep. And Amelia Rose definitely needed sleep. Then again Lorelei did too.

She closed her eyes and laid her head against the wall. A bed sat beside them, but Lorelei couldn't get up while carrying the child in her arms. Lorelei wasn't that strong. And she didn't want to drop Amelia Rose, so this is where they were. They'd both sleep better though, if Lorelei could get them onto the bed.

Except she'd do anything to keep the girl asleep. Amelia Rose was exhausted and heartbroken. This had been too much for the young preteen on the brink of puberty. She was sheltered yet worldly, ever fascinated by her father's massive media enterprise, yet kept out of its day-to-day business. She was deemed too young, although the girl had a brilliant mind. Still, she spent many fun hours in her father's office, soaking up the atmosphere of his big business. She was due to inherit a sizeable portion of the company when the time came. But not until her father's passing. In the meantime, Gerard ran the business with an iron grip on its total control.

Lorelei couldn't help but think that had something to do with this kidnapping. Where there was big money … someone was always trying to steal it.

Footsteps sounded in the hallway. Her heart sank as she watched the doorknob turn.

The door opened again.

CHAPTER 2

T HE SAME MAN walked in, and he was accompanied by two different men—not dressed in suits, like some of the others, yet not in combat uniforms either, like some of the rest. They wore jeans and T-shirts, and they gently swept Amelia Rose from Lorelei's arms and laid her down on the bed.

Half expecting them to do something horrible, Lorelei scrambled to her feet and raced over, hoping they wouldn't separate them. Amelia Rose had been through too much. These men, or maybe the other men—she no longer knew who was who—had killed Nurse in front of them after holding Mary captive and beating her. She was harmless, but they hadn't cared. Amelia Rose had screamed and cried out, struggling to get free, only to collapse in Lorelei's arms.

It had all been about lessons, making sure Lorelei and Amelia Rose learned theirs.

They'd already escaped once, hence the punishment to Nurse.

The punishment had been anything but fair.

Still, the girls had learned their lesson.

Now with Lorelei standing protectively over the sleeping Amelia Rose, the men were already backing out of the room, and the door was closed and locked behind them. Grateful for that much, Lorelei laid on the bed beside her charge and closed her eyes. She kept thinking of ways that they could escape, ways that Lorelei could get the word out again. To let Gerard know. He was powerful, had money and friends in all different kinds of places—and obviously enemies too.

It wasn't even thinkable that something like this had happened. Gerard was supposed to meet them at Island Retreat, a favorite resort where they'd planned a family holiday. Well, except not with Wendy, Amelia Rose's mother. But Gerard—or Poppy, as Amelia Rose called him—would join them. The girl had been beside herself with joy. She loved her poppy. Lorelei and Amelia Rose had come a few days early with Nurse, and then they'd been snatched up and moved to a different hotel.

They'd all escaped soon afterward, but Nurse had ordered the two girls to go one way, and Nurse would go another, hoping all would find help and would gather later today. Yet when Lorelei and Amelia Rose had returned to their original hotel, they found Nurse Mary held there as a prisoner. It had gone downhill from there.

Now they were in this new hotel. At least Lorelei assumed it was a hotel since she could see green foliage everywhere out the window. They were in a decent-size room, and it had that hotel feel to its sheets—which made a noise when you laid down. The beds were solid though, almost too solid to be comfortable.

As she lay here on the bed, Amelia Rose sniffled in her sleep and reached out in a panic.

Immediately Lorelei wrapped her arms around her charge and whispered against her ear, "It's okay. You're fine."

Only when Amelia Rose took a deep, tremulous breath and sank back into a sound sleep could Lorelei do the same.

THEY ARRIVED TWENTY minutes to noon, Thai time. Right on schedule. After a mixture of military transportation—flights, speedboats, cruisers, and helicopters—Griffin was here, and Jax was still with him. It's a good thing they'd eaten well at the beginning because food had been scarce afterward as they had been secreted away for most of their travels.

They had no instructions as they were dropped off on a wharf in one of Thailand's poorest areas. With their duffel bags over one shoulder, the two of them strode ahead to find a place to make their headquarters. They hadn't gone ten feet when Griffin's phone buzzed. He pulled it out and found an address texted to him. He checked it out online, lifted it so Jax could see what came up, and then hit the Map icon on his cell. The location was two miles ahead and down about six blocks. Both of them set off in the direction of their next stop. As they walked up to the address, they found a tourist-type hotel.

Griffin frowned. It wasn't their usual place. The two walked inside to see several clerks busy with tourists checking in. A man from a side office stepped forward and motioned for them to join him. They walked in, sat down on the chairs, and gave him hard glances while he shut the door, and no one ever exchanged a word. The fake IDs were handed over. The man quickly typed away on his keyboard, printed off several forms, and gave them keys. "Here you go, Mr. Honeycutt. Mr. Harris."

Then he opened a safe and handed a stack of money in the local currency to each of them. After that, he got up, opened the door, and sent them on their way. "Enjoy your stay."

Stuffing the money in their pockets and holding the keys in their hands, they followed the man's instructions up to their two rooms. They entered both, dropped their bags, and Griffin unlocked the connecting door. Jax pulled out a small device from his duffel bag and quickly scanned both rooms. He nodded. "They're clean."

"Interesting," Griffin said. He looked around, instinctively checking corners for video cameras and anything that might have passed the bug detector. As much as they tried to stay up on technology, it was hard to. Especially when it came to anything available in North America because China was often way ahead. He walked over to the window and took a look at the streets outside. Their beds were turned down, as if the men were ready to sleep, but it was just after noon, so that wouldn't happen.

"Do we have any intel on timing or where our kidnap victims are located?" Jax asked.

Griffin shook his head. He sat down at the table and pulled out his laptop. "We need food too."

Jax nodded. "I'll scrounge up some."

Griffin raised one finger, thinking about it, and then said, "Get enough so we don't have to go back out today for more."

"Are you hoping to make a move on her today?"

"I want to do some reconnaissance tonight," he said. "In the dark, after we have a chance to get a better location of where she is. If an opportunity presents itself, then we'll take it, but that's not likely."

"We can do that," Jax said. "I might do a little bit of looking around myself while I'm out."

"Do that," he said. Just then his phone buzzed. Jax

stopped while Griffin looked at the latest message. "Check your phone. Make sure you got these photos."

The photos were a new set, more up-to-date, of both the girl and the tutor, plus a less clear photo of the nurse.

Jax checked his phone and said, "Got it." Then he quickly disappeared out the door.

Griffin pulled up the Mavericks chat window and typed into the box. **Intel on kidnappers' location? We've landed.**

He searched online for histories on the victims, the people they were looking for, starting with Amelia Rose, who was probably the main target for the kidnappers, given who her father was. The one thing about intel was, you never knew what was important until you found it. Not a whole lot was to be found on any of these three kidnap victims—a strategic move on the part of Gerard, for sure—but then a link popped up in his chat.

He quickly clicked on it to see full background files on Mary, the nanny, Amelia Rose, and Lorelei, the tutor, completely making his last ten minutes spent online useless. In these reports, he had everything from birth date to favorite color and the outfit the little girl wore when kidnapped, as well the private school she once attended and the reason why she had a nanny and a tutor now. Apparently there had been an incident at her private preschool, and she'd been tutored ever since. She appeared well-adjusted and intelligent, though on a short leash by her protective father.

He opened the chat window asking for any updates as he studied the photo.

The chat immediately said that Mary's body had been found at the hotel where the three had gone missing.

He sucked in his breath as he stared at that message. A murder upped the stakes to critical. And why her unless she was going to hamper their progress. She was older and not in the best of health. That alone was going to have a huge impact on Amelia Rose. Emotionally and psychologically as the reports said she was close to both her nanny and tutor.

"Poor girl," he whispered. She was small and fair with a china-doll look and blue eyes and ringlets. He shook his head and sighed. "Yeah, that's not troublesome at all." She was the epitome of what a lot of people considered the perfect face. She had a cherubic innocence. And, for that, he had to hope the kidnappers hadn't had a chance to touch her yet.

Then he read the file on the tutor. She was part of a marine family and had gone her own way to become a teacher.

"At least you're not part of the Mensa group," he said. "That would be a little bit too much to handle a second time around." He'd gone a lifetime without meeting anybody with an IQ like the two people in their last case. It was fascinating, but, at the same time, as he read through Lorelei's folder, he had to wonder if she was just as brilliant, also a genius, but who had simply never been tested. She was fluent in three languages but could read and speak in five.

"Still not all that incredible," he said, downplaying it. He could handle three languages himself, but that was it. Plus, so many people born in European countries were multilingual and never thought anything about it. However, she also was licensed to teach in the arts and sciences. Her file spelled out all her upper-level university work and diplomas received.

"Interesting," he muttered as he kept going through the update. And that's when he found what he was looking for. After all her degrees had been earned, the last one as she had turned twenty-three, a big hole appeared in her background history, until she moved from the States to England seven years ago, when she was twenty-five. Followed by confirmation of her hire by Gerard as a tutor for his daughter, some five years ago, when she was twenty-seven.

Frowning, he returned to look at Lorelei's photo and asked, "What did you do after your college graduation before moving to England? And what did you do during those first two years in the UK before hiring on with Gerard?" But then she'd been young. Maybe after graduating, she had spent a year backpacking in the States or abroad. Who knew? Or two years with the Peace Corps. Or on a church mission. Still, he shook his head. Any of those suppositions would have been unearthed by the clever Mavericks team.

He quickly went back to her file and brought up another photo of her face. It wasn't beautiful or angelic like the child's, but still Lorelei had something strikingly attractive about her. It was the determined look in her face, the stern lines to her jawbone and cheeks. This woman wouldn't be taken lightly. But she was also somebody who had plans and would go wherever her plans took her, regardless of other people's opinions. If he was less than kind, he would have said she had a stubborn tilt to her chin, as if whoever took the photo had had to coax her into sitting still long enough. And her eyes had a glint in them as if to say, "Do your worst."

And he was fascinated. *Why didn't you ever marry?* He checked her photo again. She was definitely pretty enough to catch many guys' attention. And the background check on her proved she was plenty smart. The fact that she was collateral damage in this kidnapping of Amelia Rose was one thing, but, added to that, Griffin had to rescue them both.

He couldn't lose either one of them. Lorelei was needed in order to keep the young girl in a decent mental and emotional state. The tutor could be a huge help moving forward as the child dealt with this adversity. So he couldn't just learn about one victim. He had to learn about both.

By the time Jax returned to their rooms and came over to his side with large containers full of street food, Griffin had a pretty good grasp on the two people they were going after here. So he had asked the chat box for background on the father, since his daughter's kidnapping was more than likely to target her mega-rich father. The Mavericks team had already anticipated this and sent the file immediately after his request.

The father was a little bit more elusive, but he was a newspaper mogul, used to getting his own way. As a big business owner, he was stubborn and likely arrogant as hell. This was his third marriage and his daughter was his third living child. His first marriage had produced a son, who was killed at the age of two when both father and son were kidnapped. Kidnappers never captured. Griffin stalled when he read that. *How do you ever get over that loss?*

His second marriage had produced two offspring, both sons, and they were set to take over the business. But then they were much older, already in their thirties. Gerard Whitaker was in his sixties, and, from the look on his face in the photo that Griffin had been sent, Gerard wasn't an easy man to get along with, not with his hawkish nose, stern countenance, and hard eyes.

So either his relationship with his daughter was one similar to how he'd probably raised his sons, with lots of discipline and a lack of affection, or it had been the complete opposite, and she'd been the apple of his eye. Griffin leaned toward that. He moved his laptop off to the side, smiled up at Jax, and said, "Do you have enough money?"

Jax nodded. "Yes. We're good to go. And, no. Nobody's seen the girl or women."

Griffin nodded. "It was taking a chance asking. I did find out one disturbing bit of news. The nanny's body has shown up at the hotel. She's been shot. No suspects at this time."

"Jesus." Jax stared. "I wasn't expecting that."

"None of us were," Griffin said grimly. "But it's upped the ante now. Asking about the missing woman could set off another killing."

"I doubt it, it was all very casual. That's all right," Jax said. "They showed me pictures of their kids, so I brought out the photos of the girl and her tutor. I said I was here visiting them and how proud I was of their accomplishments."

Griffin laughed. "Yeah, nothing like family pride to set in. It does make me wonder how it affected the father's sons, though, at the thought of him having another family and a daughter."

"Give me the rundown."

Griffin quickly shared the information he had found online and recapped what he had been sent and said, "I just want to make sure we can write off the sons on our list as being behind this."

"So neither of our kidnap victims are married to some political type in Thailand?" Jax asked.

"I highly suspect that any political angle has nothing to do with the kidnapping, but we can't knock anything completely off our radar at this point. The kidnappers had said that she'd been married, but is that even legal?"

"In Thailand, you can probably buy a marriage for five bucks," Jax said grimly. "And child sex workers start as young as newborns."

"So the marriage angle was about rape of a child?" Griffin's stomach twisted at the thought. "That's just sick."

"The pedophiles are. It doesn't stop them from coming over here and abusing the locals for money because they can. And here, sadly some of the parents throw their kids into the industry just to make money so they can have more themselves."

Griffin shook his head. "I know all this to be true, but I don't want to sit here and focus on them. Otherwise I'll go on a rampage and free all these child sex workers out there."

"And you know they'll just kidnap another thousand to replace them. It's a messed-up world."

"It is, isn't it?" Then he dove into the food, not stopping until he was halfway through the first carton. He slowed down and said, "*Hmm*, it's not bad."

"A couple vendors are not too far from here, so we won't starve."

"Good," Griffin said. "Just when I think that I've eaten too much, I remember Brandon, that little kid from the last mission, who never even seemed to slow down."

"Are he and his dad okay now?"

"I think so. Although the father is trying to make his business a little more formally legit."

"I'm sure Brandon and Amanda want to stay connected. They're two of a kind."

"They're more than two of a kind," Griffin said. "They're seriously two halves of the same pea. That was amazing, just seeing how much brainpower was in that room."

"Make you feel bad?" Jax asked.

"No," Griffin said. "But it was definitely daunting to see just how much these people could change the world, what cures they could create, what new IT systems could be invented …" He shook his head. "It was pretty wild being around them."

"And yet, they were normal?"

"So normal," Griffin said. "Like unbelievably normal. Like you would have no clue that they were among the most intelligent people on the planet."

"And what about our Lorelei, the tutor?" Jax asked. "Apparently she's pretty smart too."

"Yes, but big gaps are missing in her history. She has four years unaccounted for, from age twenty-three to twenty-seven. She never married, yet she's thirty-two. And pretty. Don't you find that odd? Although being a live-in tutor of an eleven-year-old kid would probably seriously interfere with dating."

"If nothing showed up in the Mavericks background check, it was probably harmless stuff back then. Lots of us make mistakes when we're young and stupid," Jax said. He lifted his head, looked at Griffin, and said, "And I would think her not being married would be a plus in your view. Didn't you do something stupid when you were young?"

Griffin nodded. "Yep, I married at eighteen because I thought she was pregnant."

"But she wasn't?" Jax stared at him, his eyebrows heading to his hairline.

Griffin smiled. "Her father might have had something to do with that quick service too."

"And how long did you stay married?"

"Well, we were together for six months, but then I got

into the navy, and, on the return from my first leave, I found her in bed with somebody else. Divorce proceedings started immediately after that, and I sent a picture to her father to let him know to get off my back as she'd already found somebody else."

Jax let out a long whistle. "Wow, bet that went over well."

"No clue if it did or not," Griffin said. "She was too young to settle down, and so was I. And the father needed to let her live her life."

"Have you seen her since?"

Griffin shook his head. "Hell no. Don't care to either."

"So you should be able to relate to Lorelei choosing not to marry young."

He nodded. "I can. Something about her set of features …" He shook his head. "I'm not sure why, but she's mesmerizing."

Jax raised his eyebrows again.

Griffin laughed. "No, not like that."

"It's always like that," Jax said with a smirk. "Kerrick was the same after seeing Amanda's picture."

"Well, I won't be hooking up with this one," Griffin said drily.

"But if she's single, and you're single …"

"Single and have been ever since," he said. "Came close once or twice but I just couldn't quite get myself to pull the trigger. Not sure why. I'm going on the assumption each wasn't the right one. But then I did pull the trigger under coercion, and she wasn't the right one either. So it'll be a long, cold day in hell before I do it again."

"Unless it's the right one," Jax said.

"Well, it won't be her," he said, pointing at Lorelei's

picture. "She looks like she wouldn't be very easy to live with."

"Or maybe she would be very easy to live with if it was the right person for her," Jax said, "but hasn't found him yet."

"Whatever," Griffin said. His phone buzzed once more, and the chat box on his laptop popped up again. He quickly reached over and hit the link. It was a picture of Lorelei and Amelia Rose walking around the beachfront in Thailand. "This is from one of the resorts less than one mile away from here," he said slowly. "Taken four days ago."

"They were free then?"

"Yes. How does that work? I thought they were taken before then."

"Either this was for their good health and a ton of guards surrounded them or they escaped."

Griffin quickly zoomed in on the image and caught the look in Lorelei's eyes. "They've escaped. *There.* She's terrified, and the little girl is barely walking on her own. She's hanging on to Lorelei so tight."

"Escaped and then recaptured?"

"Quite possibly." He quickly asked that question in the chat box, and, when the answer returned in the affirmative, he nodded. "So she did her best to get them out of there, but now they've been recaptured and will be locked down even tighter."

"Well, that's not good," Jax said. "But kudos to her for getting free."

Griffin typed into the chat window. **Location?**

We're getting a suspected location.

When it showed up one minute later, the link was a photo of guarded compound. Griffin flashed it Jax's way.

"It's well-armed," Griffin said. "Likely under heavy security."

"And how do our people know that the little girl's still there?"

Griffin typed in that question.

Chip, the chat box replied.

He sat back and looked at Jax. "That makes sense. The father probably had a microchip implanted in Amelia Rose to keep track of her, in case anybody tried something like this."

"That brings up another point," Jax said. He rose, went to his adjoining room, came back with his laptop, and typed. A few moments later, he lifted his head and said, "You mentioned this before. The father and his first-born son were kidnapped some thirty years ago. Gerard obviously survived, but his son didn't."

"Can't imagine living through that," Griffin said.

"And that explains the daughter's microchip. So now we do have a confirmed location, via the chip. That's huge. But why isn't a bigger team going in to take them out?"

"Casualties? Small team is quiet, easier to hide—just the two of us."

Jax stared at him. "I'd still feel better if we had more. Don't we have backup?"

"Let me see what we've got," Griffin said as he typed in the chat box. **Reconnaissance tonight. Any backup for the plan?**

No.

Griffin winced, and Jax's jaw dropped in horror. "None?"

"Not at the moment." Griffin shook his head.

"What about Kerrick?"

"Right. I forgot he was supposed to play a part in this."

He typed in **Kerrick?**

That's me.

Wish you were here, buddy.

Paris.

Damn.

Sorry.

We need somebody else.

Let me check availability and proximity.

"Kerrick's on the other end of this chat," Griffin said with a smile. "That's good news. But then he's in Paris, not here, and that's the bad news."

"First things first," Jax said. "We need to set up a reconnaissance and take a look at exactly what we have for issues. I want satellite feed."

Griffin quickly requested the feed. When the link popped up a few minutes later, he shared it with Jax.

"Let's see what we're looking for," Griffin said. The compound itself appeared to be about ten acres total, had a high stone wall about eight, maybe ten, even twelve feet high all the way around the perimeter, with a walkway on the top. "Damn." Immediately he typed into the chat window **Can we narrow down the girl's location via her chip?**

No. Either her location is somehow blocking her chip's abilities or her chip can't narrow down her location.

Griffin grumbled as he showed Jax the recent chat window conversation. Then Griffin pointed at the satellite feed. "Interesting design," he muttered, while Jax sat again before his own laptop.

"Hey, the rules and regulations here are much less than at home," Jax said. "And permits are a joke."

"What permits?" Griffin studied the compound and said, "I'm seeing watch guards on each of the four corners and two dogs with handlers."

"I'm seeing a third pair, a dog and his handler, in the back north corner at forty-five degrees."

"Got him. So, three dogs, three handlers, and four guards." He sat back, looked at Jax, and grinned. "That's not a bad ratio. Seven men to two?"

"Make that eight, if the three dogs count as one man, if not more," Jax said, "but definitely doable."

"The trick is, we can't be seen. Not per the Mavericks contact guy and not for our general health and not for the success of this rescue op. Yet no trees are around that wall. Scaling it won't be a problem, but somehow we have to get up without any of the guards seeing us and none of the dogs smelling us."

"And getting up won't help if we're not planning on going in."

"Right. We don't want them to detect us when we're just in recon mode and then double up security before we get our rescue plan organized and put into effect. The house itself looks like it's ten thousand square feet roughly."

"Bringing up blueprints right now," Jax said, tapping his laptop keys busily on the other side of the table. "Hard to say where the prisoners are located in this mausoleum though."

A beep had Griffin checking the chat box.

Nobody local available. You guys are on your own tonight.

Griffin groaned, pointed at his drop-down chat box message for Jax's benefit.

"It is what it is," Jax said.

Griffin continued to study the external layout. "There's one driveway in with double doors. Full-size, more like seen on a medieval castle. It's pretty ironic considering they have a wall, not a moat. But the wall is too short to provide an adequate defense against a determined intruder and also too thin that it won't withstand much."

"C-4 then?"

"Potentially. We could set charges on all four corners, take down the perimeter wall, but we have to make sure that somebody's already inside and uses that as a distraction to extract the girl and the tutor."

"I think we both have to go in. Two victims, one a child, we need one man assigned per victim."

"Then we have nobody on watch outside," Griffin muttered. He grabbed a pen and paper and jotted down the details.

"We don't have any time to waste either. These kidnappers have had the girl for way too long as it is."

"Potentially we do have some leeway here, as long as the girl's safely inside, and they haven't done anything more to get themselves in even deeper shit. We need to make sure the girls don't get moved again. We're losing time with each change in location made. Or, now that we have a confirmed location for them, if the kidnappers do make a move, we catch them in transit."

"Exactly."

CHAPTER 3

LORELEI WOKE TO the door opening. She lifted her head, groggy and disoriented, Amelia Rose still sleeping against her chest. A trolley was pushed into the room, and the same man who'd been here earlier motioned at it and said, "Eat." Then he turned and walked out.

She stretched, kissed Amelia Rose gently on the temple, and said, "Wake up, little one."

Amelia Rose nodded, reached up with a fist, and tried to rub the sleep out of her eyes. She opened them to look up at Lorelei and around the room, only to have tears immediately flood her cheeks. Lorelei quickly pulled the child into her arms and said, "Yes, we're still here. Yes, we're still prisoners. But we had a chance to get some sleep. Today's a different day."

Amelia Rose looked up at her, and her bottom lip trembled. Then she saw the tray. And with the precociousness of a child, she asked, "Food?"

"Yes," Lorelei said as she got up and walked over to lift the lids on the pans. It looked to be meat, vegetables, and rice of some kind. She pulled up a chair to the little trolley so Amelia Rose could sit down. Then Lorelei poured water for them both, grabbed a roll for herself, and stood on the far side. Amelia Rose immediately wanted Lorelei to sit down, but she shook her head and said, "I need to stretch my legs."

She grinned at her charge. Even with her tear-streaked cheeks, she was busy plowing into the food. "It's good that you have an appetite."

"We need the energy," Amelia Rose said.

"We do," Lorelei agreed. She walked over to the window with the fresh bun in her hand and studied the greenery outside.

"Do you know where we are now?"

Lorelei turned, keeping a bright smile on her face, and said, "No, but lots of nice trees are outside. And it's a decent-enough room. We have our own bathroom. That's something."

"Is this a new hotel?"

"I thought so at first," Lorelei said, "but now I'm wondering if maybe it's a private home."

One thing about Amelia Rose was, she didn't think like a child. She stopped, looked at Lorelei, nodded, and said, "They can't take the chance of us escaping again."

"I know," Lorelei said. "We had our chance."

"It's my fault we got caught." Immediately the tears flowed again.

"Oh, sweetheart. No, it isn't." Lorelei rushed to Amelia Rose's side. "They were looking for us. It was only a matter of time."

"I was so scared," Amelia Rose said, looking up at Lorelei and biting her bottom lip. "If I could have run, it would have made a huge difference."

It would have, but no way would she let Amelia Rose take on this guilt. "We'll be fine."

Amelia Rose nodded and kept eating. "I don't think anybody here will get a message out for us."

"Probably not, no. Particularly since I've seen armed

men who look like staff around here. If this is a private home, which I think it is, that's most likely the answer. So I'm pretty sure the people here are paid to look after us, and they won't betray the people who pay them."

"Of course," Amelia Rose said. As soon as she was done eating, she pushed the chair back and got up and walked to the window. "It's so pretty here," she said, "but I didn't know it held such darkness."

Immediately Lorelei placed a hand on the child's shoulder and gently rubbed her arm. "You know your father's looking for us," she said. "Stay strong."

"Do you think my brothers are too?" she asked in an almost muted tone.

Lorelei winced. Her brothers had been incredibly cold and standoffish all of Amelia Rose's life, as if they hadn't wanted or needed any more siblings. And Lorelei could understand their point. But it would've been good if they could have let a little girl into their world. This little girl could bring in the sunshine. "I think they're probably rethinking their whole world right now," Lorelei said. "And you know your mother must be missing you terribly."

Amelia Rose's bottom lip trembled again. "Then why didn't she come with us?"

Lorelei didn't know what to say. Although the girl's mother did love her daughter, she wasn't the maternal type. And traveling to Thailand at this time of year had not been on Wendy's list of things to do. "I'm sorry. I'm sure she was just busy."

"She's always busy," Amelia Rose muttered. "That doesn't make it right."

"No," Lorelei said, "it doesn't, but it doesn't make it wrong either. She knew that you would be with me."

Amelia Rose nodded, squeezed Lorelei's fingers, and said, "So is this where we stay now? I really could use a computer."

"Well, you might *want* a computer," Lorelei said gently, "but I doubt they'll let us have access to the outside world. Obviously we'd try to send emails to escape again."

"I know, but I do love my games, and they're a great way to pass the time." She returned to the food trolley and said, "Do you think anything else in here is edible?"

Lorelei laughed. "Normally you like trying foods in other places of the world."

"Only if I know what they are."

Lorelei lifted the rest of the lids from the dishes so that Amelia Rose could see. "There's cake, cheese, and fruit," she said. "What would you like?"

"I'd like a pot of tea, and I'd like some cake and fruit."

There was a shelf below, and Lorelei bent to take a closer look and cried out in delight. "It looks like a pot of tea. It might be a bit strong though because we didn't see it right away." She pulled out the tea tray and set it on the floor. There were no dressers or night tables in this room. Nothing but the bed and now the trolley. She quickly cleaned off the dishes atop the trolley, then lifted the tea tray there. "And you know what? If we had thought of this earlier, it looks like this comes up." She quickly pulled a swinging shelf, topped by a sheet of wood, and locked it underneath with the proper brace.

"That would help," Amelia Rose said with a laugh. Sitting down again, they had tea and dessert.

They were almost done when the door suddenly opened again. Three men came in, and immediately Amelia Rose jumped off her chair and threw herself into Lorelei's arms.

Lorelei smiled at the men and said, "Thank you for dinner."

One of the men nodded, and the cart was taken away. Then, without hesitation, the door was slammed in their faces.

Amelia Rose looked up at her and asked, "Are they gone?"

She hugged her gently and whispered, "Yes, they're gone."

"I don't like them." Amelia Rose stepped away, looked around, and said, "At least they didn't starve us. But I really wish I had a computer."

"Or at least some books to read or a puzzle to do?" Lorelei teased. She wasn't sure what to do with her charge. It was one thing to sleep eight hours in the day and to spend another hour eating, but that left an awful lot of hours left to do nothing. The room was bare except for the single bed.

Amelia Rose looked over at Lorelei and then walked up to the door and turned the knob.

When the door opened easily, Lorelei raced to her side. A guard stood there. He frowned and slammed the door shut.

"So," Amelia Rose said with a pouting face, "I guess we don't get to leave."

"No, of course not," Lorelei said gently. "But you knew that."

"I know, but I had to check."

And, of course, Lorelei should have done that earlier too. She'd already assumed that they were under guard. Just then she stepped around Amelia Rose, opened the door, and smiled at the guard. "Is there any chance we could have some books or a computer or some games to play to fill our time?"

He frowned at her and shrugged.

"If you could ask, that would be lovely." And then she closed the door herself so that he wasn't forced to do so to keep them inside. After that, she walked to the bed, sat down, and opened her arms. As Amelia Rose piled onto her lap, Lorelei said, "Now we sit and wait."

"I'm really glad you're with me."

Lorelei's heart broke, and she held her charge closer. "I am too."

"Do you think Nurse is in heaven?"

"Absolutely she is," Lorelei said. "That's where all the good people go, and Nurse was a very good person."

"She loved me," Amelia Rose said, tears once again forming in the corner of her eyes.

"I know she did," Lorelei said. "And you loved her. And it's always hard to lose anybody so loved."

"She shouldn't have had to die that way," Amelia Rose said. "She didn't want to come on this trip in the first place."

Unfortunately that was all too true. But Amelia Rose's mother had insisted. As long as Wendy wasn't here, Amelia Rose was to have all the people who she cared about with her. Especially when she couldn't have the ones who she really loved with her, like her mother and her father.

IT WAS ONE thing to look at the compound on satellite, and it was another thing to stand in the shadows and assess the height of the wall. Twelve feet was what they'd measured off, but it was a sheer twelve feet. It looked like a smooth coat of cement on the outside. They could probably do a run and jump up and over it, but doing it quietly and silently in the night might not be quite so easy. Ropes would work though. But grappling hooks were hard to keep silent. They'd need a cover sound to be effective in close quarters like this.

The walls were smooth, but he saw gates every two yards, with small windows cut into each. *Could work with that.*

Jax tapped Griffin's shoulder and pointed off to the side.

One guard walked across the top of the wall. No railings were up there, so the wall had to be at least two feet wide for him to make that journey as casually as he did. The fact that he walked with a rifle over his shoulder said a lot about how the community would view the owners of the compound. As nobody to mess with.

Griffin watched as the guard walked around the perimeter wall, timing him. Twelve minutes for a three-quarter turn, where he met up with somebody else climbing the opposite side of the wall. Griffin and Jax had satellite images on their phones to sync with the reality on the ground while they searched the area. Two people were on the wall, two on the ground walking one dog each. Griffin hadn't seen all three dogs and their handlers patrolling yet.

The two of them moved silently in the night, taking a good assessment of what challenges and weaknesses they faced here. When they slipped back around to the far side, a large clump of trees was close enough to the wall that they could scale the trees and potentially get up on to the wall to take a look inside the compound.

As Griffin assessed the distance to the wall, he noted that the kidnappers had completely missed this weakness. In fact, it was something that, if it were up to him, he'd have fired his man over.

The tree had grown up tall and straight but had also

branched out at the top. While maybe the kidnappers had assumed that nobody would cross the wall because no branches were close enough, Griffin was high enough that, from his perch, he could drop down onto the wall. He shook his head at that.

Hearing an owl call in the night, he twisted to look at Jax in another tree, pointing to the north.

Griffin checked it out to see one of the dogs sniffing along the inside edge of the wall.

No handler was with him.

Using his night vision binoculars, Griffin checked to confirm a holding pen for the dogs was here. So this dog wasn't on duty tonight. He was just checking out the area, minding his own business. That worked for Griffin. But it was also darn close to where he would most likely land on the wall.

Not good.

Using his binoculars again, he carefully assessed the windows on the building closest to him. Several smaller buildings were inside the compound as well, but he had no way of knowing where the girls were being held. Intel said they were here somewhere, but, so far, he and Jax had no proof to back that up.

This closest building in front of Griffin had six windows accessible, where he could see how the people lived and worked inside. In one window a man sat at an office desk, talking on a phone. In another was a guard. At least he looked like a guard since a weapon was over his shoulder. He was having a cup of coffee as he stood and stared out into the night.

Not wanting him to get an instinctive feeling of being watched, Griffin quickly changed his view to check out the other windows. Two of the windows showed nothing, while one revealed a hallway all the way down as far as he could see. The question was, were the girls in this part of the building or in another area of this same huge building, or were they in one of the smaller buildings?

When the owl hoot came again, Griffin glanced once more at Jax to see him holding up his phone with a satellite image on the screen. Griffin quickly pulled out his cell and checked his satellite feed to see several men walking from one of the smaller buildings to the largest one.

He nodded. That would be the guardroom they were leaving. And that likely meant that Amelia Rose and Lorelei were housed in the bigger building.

Griffin sighed. They had at least ten thousand square feet of building to search. That would take time. They needed a way to narrow the search area. Infrared would be lovely. He frowned and sent a text. **Need infrared or better to find out where the prisoners are being kept inside the building.**

Not the usual request. Not available in that area. Will let you know.

He pocketed his phone and slipped back down, then headed to the north corner. A few trees were over here, not as big or as easy to hide in but strong enough so he could certainly scale them. On his way, he heard a dog bark. He froze, dropped to the ground, and waited. He could hear voices but saw no flashlights or heard any sounds of movement coming toward him.

When it was silent again, he moved quietly in the night and made his way to the other trees. He chose the tree with the most coverage and scaled it to the top. From his new vantage point he checked out the activity on this side of the building. Once again, he found windows that let him into little corners of the compound's world.

At one, he saw a woman staring out, but it didn't mean it was the woman he was looking for. Her features were too indistinct due to the many small panes in the window. If it had been daylight, he might have had a better look. But through the binoculars? He was just getting a female shadow.

He studied her features to see long hair and watched as she rubbed her temple. Then, hearing something, she spun quickly and disappeared from his sight. Those were good signs that maybe she was Lorelei. He mapped the location in his head and turned to study the rest of the people on this side of the building. The guards were doing their pass yet again atop the perimeter wall. Griffin stopped, checked on his timing, and nodded. Then he muttered, "At least they're consistent."

He waited another ten minutes for them to complete their pass and to see if the woman would return to the window, but she didn't. If Griffin could make it from this tree to the wall, he could quickly jump off the wall and get into the compound from that spot, then use this as a way out again. But that only worked for him doing further recon. He couldn't expect the woman and the child to make this climb. Plus the trees weren't close enough on this side to help him get onto the wall, but it would be a good area for somebody to stand guard. With that in mind, he quickly dropped to the ground and headed deeper into the trees and away from the compound.

Jax joined him very quickly. "Thoughts?"

"The best option would be to get in and to get out without waking up or having the guards notice," Griffin said.

Jax had his hands curled as fists as he glared back at the

compound. "Except they've got the dogs running free right on the side of the wall that we're likely to climb."

"Yes, and chances are those dogs will be trained to not take any gifts from strangers. We can't drop steaks in there."

"And a dog'll hear our every move."

"True, but will the dogs know us from the guards? Maybe instead of avoiding the guards, we should take out the two on top of the wall, put on their uniforms, and go in that way."

Jax thought about that and nodded slowly. "We don't know how they're getting up and down either."

"I think I saw a ladder on the inside of one of the walls," Griffin said. "It would make sense. Fast up and fast down."

"No railings to help us get up and over otherwise."

"The trees will give us access from this side, so, if we can use a ladder once inside to climb the wall out again, we'll be fine. To take out the guards, we'll need some equipment with us. And if we run into trouble inside …"

"I have a backpack with C-4 and some weapons," Jax said. "Do we know if the girls are ambulatory?"

"No clue," Griffin said. "I did see a woman in one of the windows. When somebody made a noise, like it was behind her, she quickly spun and disappeared."

"That's promising. What floor?"

"Third."

"Of course. The building won't be easy to scale from the outside."

"No, and I've seen no decks on the third floor either. There are some on the second but not above."

"So where do you want to go in?"

"I was thinking the one side door between the two tree points."

After that, they spent an hour looking for exits. Not just one but four different ways. By the time they made it back to their hotel rooms, they crashed.

Griffin woke four hours later to hear his phone buzz. He reached over, groggy.

No luck with infrared. Not a problem now that they're being moved.

"Shit," he said, sitting up. **Where and when?**

Now. To an unidentified location.

Time to overtake them?

No. Already leaving compound.

Are we tracking? He wiped the sleep from his eyes, quickly threw on some clothes, and grabbed his laptop.

Yes, satellite.

I'm on it if you've got a link.

He was given a link in an instant. He brought it up to see the satellite feed, showing the moving vehicle.

Do we have a destination?

No.

How many?

Woman, child, two men.

Including driver?

Yes.

We need a place to take them out, he said as he studied the feed.

Trying to set it up now. A blockade?

Didn't a second vehicle go with the gunmen? He hated to think about it but had to consider it.

No. We didn't see a second vehicle. You must have been seen.

No. He refused to believe that he'd triggered any alarms and that the kidnappers were leaving with their victims because of anything Griffin and Jax did. **Must be moving**

them daily. But, of course, it was possible, so he couldn't discount it. **We need wheels.**

Already on the way.

Just then an envelope was shoved under the door. He got up, walked over, and picked it up to find a set of keys. He smiled and muttered, "Kerrick's good."

Then back at the chat window, he typed **Got the keys.**

Good.

You're damn fast.

And you've been sleeping. Otherwise you'd have been on this.

He frowned. **Still had to grab some shut-eye. Can't run all the time.**

I know. That's why we've got your back.

At that, Griffin settled back and smiled.

Jax woke up, sat upright, and asked, "What's up?"

Griffin looked his way. "Looks like we wasted our time earlier doing recon. They're moving the girls."

Jax immediately bolted from bed and dressed. "Let's go."

"Go where? We're tracking them but have no clue where they're heading."

"Doesn't matter. As long as they're on the road, they're weaker than when they're in a stronghold."

Griffin laughed, throwing his duffel over his shoulder. Everything was already packed up and ready to go. Jax groaned and grabbed his bag, then the two men headed outside. Griffin hit the button on the fob with the vehicle keys and turned toward the sound of the beep. A small truck-SUV hybrid. *That would work.* They tossed their bags in the back and were on the road within minutes. He brought up the satellite on Amelia Rose's implanted tracker and held his breath until it showed him where the kidnappers were traveling.

"We need to plot an intersection," Griffin said. "They can't drive forever. They'll need gas too, but we want to make sure they're not heading to an airport. If that's the case, we want to take them out first."

With Jax running navigation, Griffin quickly drove as instructed so he could catch up with the kidnappers, who were a good forty minutes ahead, if not an hour. But they weren't traveling fast. He, on the other hand, was really moving it. He whipped through the streets, grateful that it was still the wee hours of Tuesday morning and that the traffic wasn't heavy.

"You're gaining on them," Jax said. "Looks like they've taken a turn up ahead."

"What kind of a turn?"

"Might be a pit stop."

"Good. That'll help us to make up for some lost time."

"The kidnappers shouldn't give the girls too long out of the car," Jax said. "Probably just a bathroom break."

"They have a child with them."

"We have to pick up at least twenty miles though," Jax warned him. "So go faster."

He snorted. "This bucket won't go any faster."

"I'll find you a faster route."

"Off-road works for me." On that note, the two of them focused on moving as fast as possible and catching up with their prey.

CHAPTER 4

LORELEI STOOD ASIDE, waiting while Amelia Rose washed her hands. She'd begged for a bathroom break from their two kidnappers, who had only given in after the two females had badgered them. Now their guard stood outside the washroom. When she was done, Amelia Rose reached for a hand towel and looked up at Lorelei. "I don't want to go out there again," she muttered.

Lorelei smiled gently. "Neither do I. But I've checked here, and there's no way to get out of this room, so we have to be brave a little longer."

Amelia Rose nodded. "I know. Do you think anybody in the restaurant would help us?"

"I doubt it," Lorelei said. "It's possible, but nobody wants to get involved. Obviously these are very powerful people, and they'll make things very difficult for anybody who tries to help us."

Amelia Rose wiped her eyes and said, "All I do is cry."

"And crying is just fine. There's no shame in being afraid."

"Maybe not but you're not crying."

"Inside, I am," Lorelei whispered.

Amelia Rose reached out and clung to her, clasping her hand.

"Let's go before they come in here."

As they stepped out, one of the men stood in the hall-way, waiting for them. He glanced at them, did a cursory look inside the ladies' room, and then motioned for them to go ahead.

"May I get a glass of water, please?" Amelia Rose asked.

He frowned and glanced at Lorelei, who nodded and said, "A couple bottles of water would be helpful."

He shrugged and motioned them back toward the vehi-cle. But he did say, "I'll see."

She smiled and nodded. "Thank you. It'd be appreciat-ed. Oh, and she might need food soon too."

He nodded but said, "Not yet. We're arriving at another place soon."

"Okay," she said. She led the way to the vehicle, her gaze searching around without making it seem she was looking too much. Dawn's light came over the horizon. The café was empty except for a couple rough-looking guys. She figured they wouldn't help her out. As a matter of fact, they were more likely to help out the driver and their guard instead of her. She motioned for Amelia Rose to head to the car. They walked over slowly. The driver waited for them outside, standing by the vehicle, pumping gas it seemed. He opened the car door, and they got inside.

Lorelei smiled at him and thanked him. She figured be-ing polite and friendly couldn't hurt. It might make the difference between having their faces smashed in or not. Yet this violence could happen whether they liked it or not, whether they were nice or not.

Amelia Rose snuggled up closer. "Why are they doing this?" she whispered.

"Likely because of your father and his businesses," Lore-lei said in a low tone. "He's very powerful. That means he's made a lot of enemies."

"But I haven't," Amelia Rose said in a voice that almost broke Lorelei's heart. "I haven't done anything mean to anybody."

"And that's good," Lorelei said. "We'll keep it that way, okay?" Lorelei smiled at her charge and whispered, "It's all right. We'll just stay friendly and do what we're told, and we hopefully will get out of this without anyone else getting hurt."

The trouble was that, as she stared down at her charge, curled up against her body, she knew avoiding further violence wouldn't be so easily done as said. This was bad news all around, and she had no clue who or if anybody gave a damn. As she stared out into the rising morning sun, she thought it was Tuesday, but time was hard to track in her mind. She'd never felt lonelier or more terrified.

And then she caught sight of another vehicle parked off to the side, in front of the restaurant area, the two men inside that car seemingly studying her. She frowned, trying to figure out who they were. One of the men got out and walked casually toward the restaurant. He stepped inside, and she wished she was still inside. At least he might have helped them. He looked like some badass warrior. There was a can-do attitude about him that she really appreciated. At least, if nothing else, he'd be the kind of person who would stop the others in the restaurant from hurting her and her charge. She leaned forward to speak to the driver, who still stood out front, manning the pump while filling the car with gas.

"May I go into the restaurant and get some food for Amelia Rose?"

He frowned at her and shook his head.

"Please. She needs food for the trip."

"We won't be that long," the driver said, his tone brooking no argument.

Her shoulders sagged. "Coffee? May I buy you some coffee?" He looked at her, and his gaze slid toward her hand. She held up a little bit of money that she still had from her pocket. "I don't know how much this will buy," she confessed, "but maybe a snack and some coffee for us all?"

He hesitated, but she hopped out of the car and said, "I'll leave Amelia Rose with you. Obviously I'm not escaping, leaving the child behind."

He relented and said, "My partner's inside, so don't try anything funny. Otherwise you won't see her again."

Amelia Rose hopped out. "She can't take me with her?"

The driver grabbed her arm, shuffling Amelia Rose back inside the car.

Lorelei smiled at her. "I'll return in a moment. Getting coffee and water."

Then she ran inside. At the cashier station, she quickly ordered coffee and a couple bottled waters and picked up what looked like some fresh bread from this morning plus a bag of treats for Amelia Rose. As they made up her order, she glanced around, her gaze catching the man who had just walked in ahead of her. He stared at her with a raised eyebrow. A question was in that gaze, like he was asking her if she was all right. She just didn't know how to give him an answer. She subtly held out one hand in a thumbs-down signal, as in *No, I am not all right.*

He walked toward her, and, while her coffees were being served, he ordered coffee for himself as well. "Is the coffee any good here?"

She looked up at him and shook her head, trying not to

attract her guard's attention.

"Interesting," he murmured.

"Help me, please," she whispered.

He nodded. "It's on the way."

She wasn't sure what he meant by that. Just then the driver called for her from outside. She looked over, smiled, and quickly scooped up the coffee that the cashier had just placed into the holder for her and showed it to the driver outside and to the nearby guard. She waited for her change and raced out with her guard, all the while the driver still busily yelled at her about her recent activities, but she could barely understand.

When he was done, she smiled and said, "Thank you for this." Then she handed him a coffee.

He still growled.

She handed the guard one too and then got into the back of the vehicle with her charge. She got water for Amelia Rose while Lorelei had a coffee for herself. She still had some change left in her hand, which she stuffed into her pocket. She quickly gave Amelia Rose her treats and one of the fresh rolls, grabbed another roll for herself, and then handed the bag of food to the occupants in the front seat. It was snatched from her hands. She knew they weren't happy with her, but this was a small gesture to make things a little easier.

Then she sank into her seat, wondering who the hell that man had been and if he had meant what he said. As if understanding how disturbed she was, Amelia Rose grabbed her fingers and squeezed hard. She looked down at her and saw the worry in the girl's eyes. Lorelei smiled at her and said, "It's all right, sweetie. Remember. We'll be okay."

Amelia Rose sat back and munched away as the car pulled away from the combination café and gas station and drove onto the main road. She didn't know how long they kept driving afterward. And, for the first time in a long time, she felt a whole lot better. She didn't know who that man was and what his role in all of this could be, but he'd understood that she was in trouble. That was more than she could have hoped for. Now she just had to wait and hope for an opportunity. She wasn't sure why the newcomers hadn't done anything about this at the restaurant. Then maybe it wasn't the best location? For instance, the fact that he didn't know for sure that she was even in trouble. But he knew now, so hopefully he could find a way to contact somebody to help.

She settled back and whispered, "Have a nap and rest."

Amelia Rose handed over the last of her treat and said, "I don't want this." She had a sip of water and then stretched out on the seat behind her and closed her eyes.

Not wanting the food to go to waste, Lorelei quickly polished off the last few bites and drank her coffee. She watched the two men in the front seat. They were talking, but their voices were low. She couldn't see anything. She shifted slightly so that she leaned against the far corner of the back seat but couldn't really see behind her. Shifting a little bit, she could look around the countryside as they drove. She had no clue where they were or where they were going. Only as they went around a corner did she catch sight of another vehicle far behind them.

It was the man from the restaurant.

He had believed her. Her heart lit with joy, but immediately she got worried. What if the Good Samaritans were found out? What if her driver saw they were being followed? Would they blame her? Punish her? Like they had Mary? She hoped not because Amelia Rose would have to witness that too.

She hoped it wouldn't be as bad as what they'd done to Nurse Mary, but she couldn't stop her fingers from clenching. These weren't the same men who had tortured and then killed Nurse, but the memory of what they'd done to that innocent old woman would fill Lorelei's nightmares for years. She tried to relax, slowly taking deep breaths, trying to unwind, but just knowing somebody was behind them, that somebody was looking out for them was a ray of sunshine to her heart. In her mind, she whispered to the unknown man, *Please find a way to help us. Please.*

When a shout came from the driver, she leaned forward to see him avoiding a traffic accident up ahead. He hit the brakes hard, and Amelia Rose woke up, crying. She rolled half off the seat, and Lorelei immediately grabbed her to stop her from banging into the driver's seat. The men in the front seat were cussing and swearing, but four vehicles were at odd angles across the road, two of them badly smashed.

Lorelei cried out in shock when she saw how extensive the damage was. She couldn't understand their language, but the men were talking constantly over and around her. The driver seemed to want to keep driving, but the road was completely blocked, giving him no place to go. The guard in the passenger seat got out, walked up to the accident scene, and argued with somebody on the road. Two of the vehicles were being moved off the road so the traffic could keep moving, at least in one lane.

She looked back to see the vehicle from far behind had now pulled right up to their vehicle's bumper. Her driver yelled and shouted from the window at the people hindering their path. Swiveling, she checked the vehicle behind her again. It was now empty. Both its driver and passenger were nowhere to be seen. Then she caught sight of brown hair before it sank down behind her car window. She glanced at Amelia Rose, who sat up with tears in her eyes as she stared at the accident in horror. Lorelei pulled her close. With her tight against her side, she whispered, "Be ready. This might be our chance."

Amelia Rose's jaw dropped, and she whispered back, "Now?"

"I don't know," she said, "but I want you ready, and I don't want you to cry out. And I don't want you to argue. When I tell you to run, you stay close to me. Do you hear me?"

Amelia Rose nodded.

Just then the driver opened his door, got out, and yelled at someone ahead of him.

The brown-haired man now popped up again, motioning for Lorelei to come to him.

Sitting on the far side, she silently opened her door, slid out and kept low, urging Amelia Rose to join her, then bolted backward toward the other vehicle. She came face-to-face with the man from the restaurant, and, before she could say a word, she was picked up and moved into the back of the second vehicle, Amelia Rose with her, both of them trying to stay out of sight when a blanket was thrown over them. Then the man hopped back in, and his buddy turned on the engine.

She kept Amelia Rose huddled low with her. She was darn grateful to be driving away from her captors, but what if these men were worse? She twisted upward, poked her head out, and whispered, "Do you think we're safe now?"

"No. Not at all," said the man she'd spoken to earlier. "But hopefully we will be soon."

GRIFFIN KEPT A warning hand on the girls' heads, whispering, "Stay low. Stay low."

Jax was at the wheel. He'd slowly backed up, turned around their car, and drove away, trying not to make it look like he was escaping, but, in truth, they were not only escaping but doing it as fast as possible but inconspicuously. As Griffin turned to look behind them, the two men returned to their car, only to stop and scream and yell at each other as they realized the girls had vanished.

"Now they know they're missing," Griffin said. "Pick up the speed a bit but not to draw any real attention."

Jax already had goosed his gas pedal, waiting for Griffin to give him the all clear to get this vehicle in high gear.

As Griffin watched, the other vehicles now joining in this traffic jam had pulled up behind the kidnapper's vehicle, effectively boxing them in, filling in the void their leaving had opened. Another one pulled out of the row and turned around, doing what Jax and Griffin were doing, rather than waiting for the vehicles in the accident to clear off. It effectively jammed in the kidnappers' car.

"They're on their phones, calling for help," Griffin said, "since they can't get out of the traffic jam."

"Good," Lorelei snapped from behind the front seat. "They deserved that."

When they rounded a bend in the road that cut them off from the kidnappers' sights, Griffin told Jax to floor it.

Jax put the pedal to the metal, but then he coaxed it up another gear. "Let's hope we have enough of a head start."

Griffin leaned over his seat and looked down at the two girls. Lorelei's eyes were brown and wide, filled with a bit of temper and a little bit of uncertainty. But Amelia Rose's eyes broke his heart. She was clearly terrified. He smiled at her and whispered, "It's okay. We're the good guys." But it didn't look like his words had any effect. He looked at Lorelei. "Do you know what they wanted from you?"

She pointed toward Amelia Rose. "They want her."

"We heard from your dad," Griffin said gruffly. "So, Amelia Rose, you'll be okay. We just have to get you to safety."

At the mention of her father, her eyebrows rose, and her eyes widened. "Did Poppy send you?"

"In a roundabout way, he did," Griffin said, not having a clue who was behind his orders. "The bottom line is, we were sent to rescue you and to get you out of here safely."

"I'm not going without Lorelei," Amelia Rose said, her tone stubborn.

Griffin chuckled. "We're taking both of you." He kept an eye on the road behind him. "Looks like we've lost them for the moment, but I'm sure they've radioed ahead. We have to switch vehicles."

Just then his phone buzzed. He glanced down to read an address, punched in for the map, and held it up for Jax.

Jax looked at it and nodded.

Griffin typed in the address into the car's GPS. As soon as Jax understood where the address was, Griffin wiped the GPS from their car and from his phone. Griffin then forwarded the image he'd taken of the kidnappers' license plate to his Mavericks contact. They should be able to track the car and, with any luck, the drivers.

"Can they really track your car, your phone, see your recent activity?" Lorelei asked in confusion, having seen what Griffin had done.

"We don't want to take the chance that they can," he said. "Worse than that is if they're tracking us via satellite."

She stared at him in horror and then cried out, "We

have to ditch this vehicle."

"Like I said," he said, "we have to switch vehicles."

Just then they went through a series of turns as Jax took the vehicle on a roundabout trip and pulled into a parking lot. There wasn't much in the way of decent vehicles here, but Jax obviously had a plan. He headed to the far side where two vehicles had pulled up beside each other. The men stood off to one side, arguing something fierce, and they didn't notice Jax slide into the driver's side and take off with one their vehicles toward Griffin and the girls.

"Move," Griffin said, "now." He was out and opening the door to assist Amelia Rose. Lorelei was already out on Jax's side. She had yet to notice that there was no sign of Jax. She came racing around to Griffin's side of the vehicle and held out her arms. Amelia Rose ran into them.

Their new transport pulled up; they dashed inside and hit the road. Griffin watched behind them again, but neither man, still intent on their argument, had yet to notice that one of their cars had been stolen. A few blocks later he smiled and said, "Clear." He turned to face the girls in the back seat. "Now"—Griffin pulled the armband he'd been carrying in his pocket for just this moment—"Amelia Rose, lift your right arm please."

Shocked, she slowly lifted it to rest on his seat in front of her. "Why?"

He smiled, reached around, and placed the band in the middle of her upper arm. "You have a tracking chip in your arm. This will block the signal."

She twisted her new accessory. "It should come in better colors."

He laughed. "No such luck. Black is all I've got. Don't take it off, *unless* you become separated from us. And then we'll use that signal to track you two down again. But blocking it now should stop the kidnappers from tracking you again."

"That's how they knew where we were after we escaped." Lorelei cried out, studying the new arm band. "We never had a chance."

Jax took another rough corner, sending the girls sliding along the back seat.

"Wow," Amelia Rose said. "He doesn't drive very well, does he?"

Jax snorted from the front seat. "I drive better than you think," he said. "I just have to make sure that we're not being followed."

At that, Amelia Rose stayed quiet.

Griffin looked at her and said, "My name is Griffin, and that's Jax."

She looked up at Griffin and said, "You're a winged horse?"

"Winged lion," he corrected with a big smile. "And you're Amelia Rose, and you're Lorelei, right?" When both nodded, he could feel their relief settling inside. "Now that we got that straight, I need to know if either of you are hurt." His gaze was searching as he studied the child and then the woman. He didn't want to ask if they'd been assaulted in any way, but it happened so often that he knew he had to be sure.

Immediately Lorelei shook her head and whispered, "We're both okay. I don't know for how long that would've lasted though."

"Any idea why you were being moved?" Jax interrupted.

"No, not really."

"They had to move us. To get us away from what they'd done to Nurse. She's in heaven," Amelia Rose said tearfully. "They killed her so we'd behave."

CHAPTER 5

L ORELEI STUDIED THE two men who now held their lives in their hands. She hadn't seen anything that showed her something was off with them, but, at the same time, it was hard for her to be too complacent. She didn't know them. They'd helped her and Amelia Rose escape, but who were they exactly? "Are you sure her father sent you?" she asked cautiously.

"We're special ops," Griffin said. "Her father initiated the request, but the government sent us. I doubt he knows who the two of us are personally."

"I guess I wonder which government it is," she said smoothly.

The corner of his eyes crinkled, and he nodded. "Good question. We're both American."

Lorelei's heart froze, and her eyes widened. "But her father's British."

"One of those joint task forces," Griffin said, which made Jax snort. "Except he's an American citizen."

"I'd like to see the *joint* part of this," Jax said.

Griffin turned that light gray stare in her direction. There was no deceit, but there was also no give in them. "We were given a mission, given orders to extract both of you from the difficult situation you were in. So that's what we did."

She frowned. "Orders?"

"Yes," he said, "that's how this works. We're offered a mission, and, if we accept, we're all in."

She hated to say it, but something was almost depressing about that. She hated to be just another mission; yet, if they hadn't been designated as a mission, the two of them would still be prisoners. But she nodded and said, in a more formal tone, "Then thank you."

"Don't thank us yet," Jax said cheerfully from the driver's side. "We could have gone from the soup into the stew."

She hated that analogy. She twisted to look behind them, but nothing was there. Thankfully it looked like they'd lost their kidnappers. "Well, at the moment, the kidnappers aren't behind us, so I'll take that as a blessing."

"Yes," Griffin said, "but we need to know who's behind the kidnapping. I'm not prepared to turn you over until we're sure this is resolved and the two of you are safe."

Something about his wording sent unease sliding through her. Surely they'd not hold them hostage too, would they? "Presumably you'll turn us over to our British government," she said smoothly, "so we can go home."

"Is that where you are from?" Griffin asked, testing her honesty.

She nodded. "I'm American, but I've been living in England for the last seven years, and I've been with Amelia Rose for five of those seven."

"So her father sent you to Thailand for a holiday?"

"Her mother did," she said quietly, glancing at Amelia Rose, who was still lying on the back seat and staring at the men. Lorelei nodded and added, "Just the three of us but her father was to join us there."

"They killed Nurse Mary," Amelia Rose said in a faint

voice.

Griffin stared at her and nodded. "I'm sorry, little one. It's hard to lose someone at any time, but, under these circumstances, it's much worse. We did hear that one of your party was dead. I'm sorry about that."

"They shot her," Lorelei said. "And I think it was a lesson and a warning to us to behave, or we'd follow the same suit."

"It makes sense," Griffin said. "But apparently there wasn't any ransom note. Instead they said that Amelia Rose had been married. I thought it was you, Lorelei, originally, because I didn't understand child marriages here. Still don't for that matter," he muttered under his breath.

"They're big in many parts of the world," Lorelei said. "But the fact remains, she would not ever partake of or agree to any arranged marriage at any age, and, since she is not of age, they don't have her father's permission. None of that was mentioned to us, so I doubt any intended marriage had anything to do with this. And, although they had no hesitation killing Nurse, they didn't hurt us."

"Either way, you were both being held against your will."

Lorelei gave a strong nod. "We three were originally kidnapped on the street and were taken to some hotel. When our guard was called away from the front door to our hotel room, we escaped out the patio door. We all three left but separated soon afterward. I was to stay with Amelia Rose, and Nurse was to return to our hotel room to gather our things and wait for us to meet up with her there as soon as we could.

"As we went back to our original hotel room, they were inside the room waiting for us. They already had Nurse—

Mary, but she preferred to be called Nurse. She'd gone down for a nap, and they woke her up and had her tied in a chair when we returned. They'd hit her a couple of times. Poor Nurse. I should have known better than for any of us to return to our registered hotel rooms. We were told we were to cooperate or else. Then, as a warning, they shot her—in front of us."

Griffin winced. "They probably planned on killing her anyway," he said gently. "They couldn't leave any witnesses behind."

She hated to think of that, but it had crossed her mind. She nodded slowly and said, "I'm just so sorry that her last minutes on earth were full of terror. I'm also sorry poor Amelia Rose was subjected to seeing that. She loved Nurse very much. It's traumatizing for her."

"And I'm glad that you two are not facing your last few minutes on earth right now," he reminded her. "And, with any luck, we can get you out of this mess. Her father can get a specialist to help her deal with the trauma when you are home."

That reminder Lorelei needed to keep close to her heart. They'd been through a lot already. And she wanted to trust these two men. But something devastatingly attractive about both of them made her instinctively not want to trust them either. She'd had more than her fair share of smooth slick males. Not that these guys were like that, but she didn't want to take the chance.

Amelia Rose needed to feel secure right now, and Lorelei couldn't take the chance of these men betraying them too. "We figured her father was being blackmailed," she said in a low tone. "That maybe something related to his businesses was involved in this."

"Well, Gerard has two sons and then Amelia Rose, correct?" He kept his gaze on her.

She turned to look at Amelia Rose to find her eyes were closed. Lorelei gently shifted the little girl so that her head lay on Lorelei's lap and brushed the hair off her head. "Yes," she said. "Two adult sons who run part of the business and a dad who's old enough that he's thinking about easing back, so he can spend more time with his new family."

"And sometimes that doesn't always go over well in the family," Griffin said. His tone was bleak.

She wondered what he was getting at. She understood some of his suspicions about the sons, and she had to wonder herself. "The brothers have no deep love for Amelia Rose," she said quietly. "As sad as that is, there are an awful lot of years between them. Decades, in fact, and probably not a wish to share the very hefty inheritance pot either. However, I'm not sure risking all that would be worth it to get rid of her."

"I think, at this point in time, there's probably more than enough inheritance for three."

"Probably," she said, "but some people will never have enough."

"True enough," Jax said. "We're five minutes out."

She looked around the area with interest. "And where are we going?"

Griffin shrugged and said, "To our next destination." He flashed her a wicked grin and turned to study their surroundings.

Even though he had been speaking with her, he never really lost that sense of alertness. And it was back in full force now too. She wondered if this was because of an already pretty intense scenario or if that was just the kind of guy he was. Did he work all the time? Did one take a break from this kind of a living? Was there even a break, or is that what they did until they died? Did these men die with their boots on? She had no clue, but it was an interesting thing to contemplate. He hardly looked like a 9-to-5 office-type guy.

He was obviously the one in charge here, but Jax was an equal partner from appearances. She listened as the two discussed entryways. She didn't quite understand the wording or what they meant, but her thoughts were now consumed with Amelia Rose's brothers. She had met both of them a few times. They'd been arrogant but friendly. Both of them had been born into big money, and both of them had gone to business school, rising rapidly up through the ranks of their father's company, like their father had for his father. Yet Gerard retained full control.

The sons felt they had earned their positions, whereas she was sure the sons had viewed Amelia Rose as just an observer, a pretty little tagalong who would spend money and not make it. As long as she kept to her little pile of money off to the side and just had fun on her own, the sons probably wouldn't bother with her.

Yet her father had constantly mentioned bringing her into the business when she was old enough. Maybe that was enough to set this off. Lorelei didn't know. She hoped not because how wrong would that be to be worried about your kid sister taking part of your inheritance pot when the pot was so damn big? Taking an active role in the mega-business that surely needed more bosses? But it was so hard to know what people were thinking, and sometimes they weren't thinking at all. They were just reacting.

Griffin turned suddenly and asked, "Was her mother supposed to come on this trip?"

Lorelei shrugged. "Maybe … originally. I don't know. I'm not privy to those kinds of plans."

"What kind of relationship does Amelia Rose have with her mother?"

Not really liking where this conversation was going, Lorelei pinched her lips together and tried to be detached about it. Obviously somebody was behind this nightmare, so they needed to consider everyone and everything. "They were friendly," she said, "but not necessarily very loving. Her mother is not very motherly, shall I say. Amelia Rose is closer to her father."

"So, if somebody wanted to hurt her mother, would doing something like kidnapping Amelia Rose be the worst way to do it?"

She shook her head. "No, it would be her horses."

Griffin went still, then gave a clipped nod. "And the best way to hurt her father?"

"Either his sons or Amelia Rose," she affirmed. "She and her father have a very caring relationship." She smiled. "We should all be so lucky."

"THAT CONFIRMS WHAT I was thinking, that maybe she was the apple of his eye," Griffin said, keeping his voice neutral and not letting Lorelei know exactly what he was thinking. Because, at the moment, he wasn't even sure what he was thinking himself. His thoughts were firing off in random directions, still putting the pieces together. But, one thing was for sure, the mother was a suspect, and so were both sons. Yet he highly suspected that was just the tip of the iceberg in this case. Hell, there were too many suspects at this point. Best if they could knock some off the list. He hated to think that either parent was involved.

He looked over at Jax, who pointed ahead. Immediately Griffin leaned forward to study the neighborhood. The address was the fifth floor of a high-rise. Underneath in the parking garage, he helped Lorelei out, then leaned in and quickly scooped up the sleeping child.

With the duffel bags now carried by Jax, a procession headed up to apartment 504. The door was unlocked. They stepped inside, and Griffin walked right through to one of the bedrooms and laid the little girl down. He pulled a blanket off the second bed and quickly covered her up. Then he stood for a long moment in the doorway, wondering what kind of a bastard would hurt a young girl. He didn't understand the child-marriage part of it at all.

However, in many countries, women were nothing but chattel, and marrying them off meant they had become somebody else's possession. In many cases, it was legally binding too. He wasn't sure about an eleven-year-old being of marriage age, but, having heard nightmare stories about child brides in many parts of the world, he wouldn't be at all surprised in theory. But, in this case, there was no parental permission. She'd been kidnapped. And that was the key.

She was also a British citizen, but women disappeared into the sex trade all too often. From everywhere. Hell, many were young girls too. It's possible marriage would be the end result for some but not for the majority. Boys had value but in a different sense; girls were valuable for blending marriages and powerful families. It was a scary world out there.

Griffin couldn't see that as being anything other than a punishment for the father though. Particularly if they thought that they could get him to believe she had been raped. Griffin presumed any parent would do anything to rescue their child from that scenario.

He stared down at his clenched fists, hating that, even now, the thought of child rape could disturb him so much. He'd seen such atrocities in the war and had tried to avoid coming in contact with much of it because he tended to lose his temper and take it out on anybody and everybody involved.

Griffin had gotten in trouble in the navy as a young seaman after finding out one of his colleagues had taken advantage of a Thai girl. She'd only been nine. The man in question had taken a hard beating from Griffin and then had been thrown in the brig until his trial, which all had helped Griffin deal with this issue, but it hadn't been enough. That little girl had to carry the childhood trauma of that rape for the rest of her life, and that wasn't fair.

Hating the thoughts in his mind, he walked to where Lorelei had collapsed into a recliner and crouched beside her and said, "Please tell me for sure that she wasn't raped."

Immediately Lorelei shook her head. "No, she wasn't. Neither of us were."

"Did a marriage of any kind take place?"

She shook her head. "No. They did treat us better this last twenty-four hours though. Amelia Rose was given food and water and a bed to sleep in."

"Probably realizing that a child being treated a little bit better would be easier to deal with."

"Or make her prettier," Lorelei said caustically. "It's all about the value of the child."

"But there could be all kinds of value involved in something like this," Griffin said. "Even if it's to make her father's business holdings look shaky because he can't look after his family. Stock prices on his US newspaper holdings have already started to drop."

"Why would people do things like that?"

"To make money," he said. "To make lots and lots of money."

"If someone did that," Jax said from behind her, "they would have sold their stock immediately. And now that the shares are dropping, it's pretty easy to buy up shares cheap when it hits its low point. Then you wait until they bounce back up again and sell them off for a tidy profit."

She shook her head, stood from the chair, and walked to check on Amelia Rose. Lorelei wrung her hands as she paced back and forth, obviously distressed. "The only ones I can think of who would have anything to do with this," she said, "would be either Gerard's sons—because they're part of the bigger business picture—or one of Gerard's enemies. And I'm sure he has more than a few of those."

"What's he like to work for?"

"As long as you're on his good side," she said with a wry smile, "it's fine. But the minute you cross him, like anybody, it's not much fun."

"Is he fair?"

She tilted her head to the side, thought about it, then nodded slowly. "Anytime I've had any dealings with him, it seems like he was fair. But then my job is looking after Amelia Rose, to teach her, to guide her, and to help her grow up. As long as I do that, and she appears to be in good health emotionally and physically, then he's happy with me. But, when he does test her on her knowledge, if she slips up, I'm the one who gets blamed."

"That's because the father never wants to believe the child is not doing what she's supposed to," Jax said with a smirk. "Did he ever show any signs of violence toward her or his wife?"

Immediately Lorelei shook her head. "Not that I ever saw. I'm with Amelia Rose most of the time."

"What about Nurse?"

"No," she said, her face softening. "Gerard had a soft spot for Nurse."

"And his wife?"

She winced and exclaimed, "I hate saying bad things about anybody."

"You don't have to," Jax said, his tone quiet but giving no quarter. "But, if you want to get out of this nightmare scenario and get back to England and be completely free of this threat, we need the truth."

"I would say it's a loveless marriage then," she said promptly. "I don't think they even have meals together."

"Any sign of a divorce in the offing?"

"I think Gerard's tired of divorces," she said. "He lost out pretty badly on the last one. Likely the one before that too."

"There would have been a prenup on this one though," Griffin said. "I can't believe he wouldn't have that in place."

"True," she said, "but it's also important to understand that he doesn't want to disrupt Amelia Rose's life."

"Sure. But one has to find happiness somehow," Griffin said. "I don't believe in staying together for the children. Those kids feel the tension, see the fights, the lack of real communication. It leaves a mark on them, in my opinion. And a child witnessing a bad marriage is not setting a good example for her either. Every child should be so lucky as to have two loving parents, who love and respect each other, and who love their children unconditionally."

Lorelei sighed. "There are more divorced families now than not in some places," she said with a nod. "All I can tell you is that there doesn't seem to be any affection or love between Amelia's parents."

"Do you ever see the three of them together?"

"Yes, but not often," she said, slowly crossing her arms over her chest as she stood, her legs slightly wide. She stared at the two men. "Is this really necessary?"

"Yes," Griffin said. "We have to figure out exactly what's going on, and, to know that, we have to figure out who the major players are and what their role in this is."

"I don't believe that either Gerard or Amelia Rose's mother has anything to do with this," she said. "Gerard adores Amelia Rose. As for Wendy, I don't think she wants anything to change the status quo." Lorelei held up her hand. "Let me qualify that. Wendy doesn't want to be poor. Wendy loves money and what it can buy. That's her status quo. Her status quo has nothing to do with being married to Gerard but that she married a rich man. Any rich man would do, in my opinion. She obviously has no respect for marriage as an institution—or even motherhood for that matter."

"Meaning, if she were to instigate matters, she'd have, more than likely, targeted Gerard instead of her daughter?"

"Exactly," Lorelei said. "When you think about it, she doesn't want a divorce, but that doesn't mean being a wealthy widow would be a bad thing."

Griffin nodded, walked to the window, and stared outward from one of the corners. He knew enough to not stand fully in front of the window and to let anybody even see him. He didn't know what the deal was on this apartment—who it belonged to; where the owners were; how their Mavericks boss came to know about—and it didn't matter.

It was a place to stay. He glanced at her and asked, "When did you eat last?"

"I picked up coffee and a few treats at that coffee shop where I met you," she said. "I shared them with the driver to make the relationship a little less strained, but that was our last meal."

"So you need food then?"

She nodded. "As does Amelia Rose. But we need good food, like real food."

Jax was in the kitchen, opening cupboards. When he opened the fridge, he said, "Aha."

Griffin looked at him and asked, "What did you find?"

"All the food's here, just like I asked," Jax said with a big smirk. "We got a roasted chicken, a cooked beef roast, lots of sliced deli meats, cheeses, and salad makings." He opened another cupboard and brought out bread and buns, then quickly took the food from the fridge, and they stared at the assortment.

"You guys came better prepared than I expected," she said in surprise. "This is definitely food, and it's people food. But Amelia Rose'll want kid food."

Jax nodded as he studied Lorelei. "If we stay another night together, we'll get whatever Amelia Rose wants. Just tell us what she likes."

"In the meantime, this is what's here," Griffin said. "If she's hungry, I'm sure she'll find something to eat."

CHAPTER 6

"I DON'T KNOW. I don't think it's quite that easy," Lorelei said with a smile as she walked over to see the possible choices for Amelia Rose. *Eggs, cream, and cheese.* Lorelei nodded. "She'll have a cheese omelet with this."

"Good," Jax said. "I, on the other hand, will have a huge salad with lots of protein." He looked over at Griffin. "You?"

"Absolutely."

The men prepped a large salad while she watched. She frowned because she hadn't been asked herself. When they had a load of salad mixed up with veggies in a large bowl, Griffin looked at her and said, "Are you having an omelet with her or a salad?"

"Just salad?"

"A whole roasted chicken is here," he said. "I'll chop up some on the side, like a Cobb salad or a chef salad."

She smiled. "I'll have some of that then, please."

He nodded and got back to work.

She wandered the small living room, hating the sense of not knowing what to do next. "Does her father know?"

"By now, probably yes," Jax said. "But we can't get confirmation."

"Why is that? You guys are just the leg men?"

"We're the ones who go in and get the job down," Griffin said, his voice harsh. "We leave the glory and kudos to everybody else."

She stilled, studied his face, and smiled gently. "And that's what your life's been like? Rescuing people from situations in foreign countries, and nobody even knows who you are?"

"Yes. And I'm okay with that," Griffin said. "If you do a job, you do it right. And, if you do it right, it doesn't matter who else knows."

"That's a quote I haven't heard before," she said curiously. "Where'd you get that one from?"

"From myself," he said. "It's a motto I live by."

"It's a good way to live," she said. "As somebody who's involved in raising a young girl in this world and explaining to her how all this works, it's not a bad one for her to understand."

"If it works for you," he said, "use it. But just keep in mind that a lot of people don't understand the hardships in life. We're never really challenged until life throws us some of the shittiest things. Then we have to pull up and out of it."

"So, besides the fact that you're very busy saving the world," she said, "what personal challenges have you had to suffer through?"

He looked up at her, surprised. "Do I have to have had some?"

She nodded. "Yes, I think so. Personal challenges ensure changes on a whole different level. It sounds like you've been through both."

"Maybe," he said noncommittally. He reached for the roasted chicken, cut it through the breastbone and through the back, and then deboned the breast, dissecting off the pieces. He placed everything on a plate as he worked.

She watched, realizing he was avoiding her question. "Have you ever been married?" He almost cut his finger. He swore softly, and she took that for a yes. "What happened?"

"What often happens when men are away at war," he said.

"She hooked up with somebody else?"

He nodded, glanced at Jax, but he was happy being by himself as he continued to build up the salad. He was listening to the conversation but not getting involved.

She walked closer, not sure exactly why she felt like she needed to prod, but there was just something about this man, so capable and so strong, so determined to follow his own rules. It's as if he was not looking at other parts of his life, the other areas where the rules might need to be bent slightly in order for him to have some peace inside. "So, did you just walk away then, not have any more relationships with women?"

He raised an eyebrow. "Hell no."

She chuckled. "Well, it's good to know. But you can't let one bad experience taint the rest of us. But I suspect something else in your past drives you to avoid marriage."

"Of course," he said. "But not my cheating wife. She's not worth the effort, but I've seen the hardships war has wrought on the women and children left behind and the dangers from other military men. It's not a pretty sight, and one I've seen way too often." He cleaned his hands and the knife. "But you'd be wrong to think it's made me avoid relationships. It's helped me stay focused on my career, but I've dated lots."

"True, but you didn't let yourself get too involved, huh?"

"Yes, but don't go thinking that I loved her dearly and

was totally betrayed by it," he said with a shake of his head. "It wasn't like that at all."

She frowned at him and said, "Then what was your marriage like?"

So he told her. She took a step back, shook her head. "Surely that doesn't still happen in this day and age?"

"Her father felt very strongly about it all and made it clear what I would do to fix the problem," Griffin said with a hard smile. "I have no idea how he feels about her now though."

"That was kind of a bitchy move to send him the photo but understandable," she said. "He forced you to live what— eight months of your life according to his will, so I guess it makes sense that you had a little retribution."

"Exactly," he said, "but I left that alone a long time ago."

"No, you haven't," she said. "Otherwise you could laugh at it. Instead your mouth still tenses and your shoulders stiffen when you think about it."

He stared at her with that same hard look again. "Doesn't mean that I'm not over it."

She shrugged. "But neither are you relaxed enough to go back into a relationship to that level again."

"I don't want to go into a relationship to that level," he said. "That relationship was at the surface level. It wasn't based on truth, faith, honesty, or loyalty. Why would I ever want to go back to that?"

"So, you should do something different," she said. "Something better."

"Maybe," he said, "but that's not quite so easy. One doesn't just conjure up a good relationship that can withstand the test of time."

She snagged a piece of cucumber from the salad bowl.

"True enough. And you never will if you don't put yourself out there."

At this point, Jax laughed. "What are you doing? Matchmaking on the run?"

She shrugged. "No, not really, but it's my attempt at a more lighthearted conversation that's not related to what we've just been through. So I'm more than happy to keep going with this train of thought and leave off discussing all this ugliness around us."

"Good answer," Jax said. He picked up the large bowl of salad, carried it over to the small table, and quickly handed her plates and cutlery. As she set the table, he asked, "What about you? Have you been married?"

"No," she said. "I wasn't going to jump into anything too early after watching several friends married and divorced within a couple years. Most now with young children to look after on their own as single parents. I decided that wasn't for me. However, when the time came, I fell in love hard and fast. I came close to marrying him, but I didn't get to the altar."

"Why? Did he fall in love with somebody else?" Griffin asked, his tone rough.

"He died in a rowing accident," she said suddenly, a catch in her voice. "We were in England for a holiday. It would be an extended holiday, while he considered going to school there. He was offered to join a rowing team. Anyway, he went out early one morning and didn't come home."

"Do they know what happened?"

"He was diabetic," she said, "and he got too cold, and they figured that he ended up without enough energy to make it back again, then fell into a coma and drowned."

"And are you satisfied with that explanation?"

She shot him the briefest of smiles. "It's an unhappy one but, yes, because I've seen him do it before. We used to hike a lot, and he was really crappy about looking after himself. If he didn't have something sugary to get him through, I could see him definitely falling into a coma."

"So then what did you do?"

"I stayed in England," she said. "Very soon afterward, I ended up with this tutoring position, looking after Amelia Rose."

"You could do something very different from that with your qualifications."

He watched as she hesitated and looked at him, and then she said, "And, of course, you guys have investigated me, right?"

They shrugged and then nodded.

"Right, so you already know about my fiancé, and the gaping hole in my life that he left behind brought me here," she said. "And, well, I could have done something different but was lost and needed something—someone—to love. By then, I'd already fallen in love with Amelia Rose. Back then I couldn't see leaving her too. Besides the pay is way beyond what I'd make in the public or private education system. Sure I could go into the political arena as a translator or work for the UN possibly, but, as I said, Amelia Rose gives me more love and job satisfaction than any other option I've looked at. So, whether others agree or not, I'm happy."

"What do you mean—leaving her *too*?"

"Her father had a relationship with the child's maid," she said, sitting down hard on one of the kitchen table chairs. "When the relationship was over, of course, the maid was gone. Plus that wasn't the first time. But each and every time it's another blow to Amelia Rose. She needed some stability in her life, somebody who could care for her and be there for her and not be her father's latest paramour."

"And you're not in line for that position?"

She chuckled. "No. Let's just say I prefer Amelia Rose over her father any day."

Griffin smiled at her approvingly. "See? Being single isn't so bad. And being faithful isn't bad either."

"No," she said. "I'm both of those. But it was also hard to lose my partner before, so I haven't exactly jumped back into the relationship setting too easily. I'm entitled to have a relationship, but it's not something I really want to pursue, especially not while I have Amelia Rose to look after."

"True," Jax said, "but you can't be single forever because of a child. She's eleven, and she's getting old enough to understand."

"She's getting old enough that she's pushing me into dating," Lorelei said with a groan. "She kept telling me which waiters and people at the hotel would be ideal partners for me." Both men laughed. She stood and said, "Speaking of which, I should check on her."

"I'll do it. You're tired. Just rest," Griffin said. He walked down the hallway.

Soon enough, Lorelei heard voices and realized her charge was awake.

She was about to jump up when Jax placed a hand on hers and said, "Let him."

She raised her brows at that but subsided. When she looked up again, Griffin carried Amelia Rose, the two of them smiling and laughing together. Wow. That was great to see Amelia Rose so comfortable with Griffin after the nightmare she had been through. "He's good with her," she murmured to Jax. When Amelia Rose was set gently on her feet, she raced over to Lorelei, and the two hugged.

Lorelei motioned to the chair beside her and said, "This one's for you."

She hopped up, looked at the food on the table, and frowned. "I don't like veggies."

"Don't you like to run far and fast?" Griffin asked. "You need veggies for that."

Lorelei looked up at him in surprise, wondering if he knew about how they had been recaptured.

"You need energy. You need food. You have to feed the body in order to keep the energy supplies running so that, when you need to run, you can run."

Without another word, Amelia Rose reached for the salad and put some on her plate. Lorelei helped her pick out the rest of what she wanted, some sliced chicken breast and her choice of dressing, and then, before long, she was tucking into the salad like she was an old veggie champ.

Lorelei shook her head in a slight way and told Griffin, "That's not the tact I would have used, but it was effective."

"It's also the truth," he said, "and I am a believer in being truthful whenever we can. Surely it's better for kids too."

She wasn't sure if that was a criticism or not, and, of course, he didn't know enough about Lorelei to understand the problems they had getting Amelia Rose to eat healthily. But, if Amelia Rose was finally understanding that she needed to eat better, then that was all good.

Lorelei thoroughly enjoyed her meal, but she caught herself yawning now that all the adrenaline had worn off and that they were more or less safe at the moment. She needed a good night's sleep tonight, but she didn't know how long they were staying. So far the men hadn't said anything to her about their plans. Whether that was on purpose or not, she didn't know.

Amelia Rose piped up and said, "I want to talk to my daddy."

"When we're in a safe place," Griffin said, "then you can."

"Are we not safe?" the little girl stared up at him, her bottom lip trembling.

He gripped her hand gently and said, "This is step one. We can't take a chance that somebody may have followed us here or that they're tracking our transmissions. So, when we do get to a place where we can be sure that we have a safe line, then you can talk to your father."

She nodded slowly and went back to eating.

Griffin turned to Lorelei and asked, "Is there anybody we should contact about your disappearance?"

She shook her head. "My parents would just worry, and they don't know even what I do on a day-to-day basis, so it's not an issue."

"Did they disapprove of your job?"

"Not so much disapprove as just thought it was below me," she said with a half smile. "Like you, they thought I was destined for bigger and better things."

Immediately Amelia Rose gripped Lorelei's fingers. "You're not leaving me, are you?"

"No," Lorelei said. "I've told you that before."

Amelia Rose sank back and smiled. "Good. Then I don't have to worry about waking up one day to find out you're gone too."

That too broke her heart. "I know," Lorelei whispered. "I've told you before that I won't leave without giving you lots of notice, and probably, at that point in time, you'll be ready for me to go, to give you some freedom."

Amelia Rose shook her head. "No, I can't imagine that."

"Well, you might want to go to another school and have friends your own age," Lorelei murmured. "But you never really know what opportunities may arise, what surprises your dad may have for you. Who knows? Your family might move to France or Greece. Or maybe you want to be a travel writer for your dad's newspaper someday, living in other cultures, or maybe a political writer, understanding what's going on in the world as things happen."

"Like what happened to Nurse?" Amelia Rose whispered.

"Kind of," Lorelei said, wishing she hadn't brought it up. "But there are good things in life too."

"Like what?" Amelia Rose demanded.

"Griffin and Jax, for one," Lorelei reminded her. "They saved us. We're not in the back of a car being carted off to some odd location to be watched by guards."

"That's true," Amelia Rose said as she turned her solemn and direct gaze to both men. "Thank you for that."

Both men nodded. Jax smiled and said, "No problem. Now let's make sure that they can't come after you again."

"That wouldn't be good," Amelia Rose said. "I don't know how many times anybody can escape before the odds are against you."

Lorelei watched as Griffin studied the young girl. Every once in a while, she said things that were almost too adult. She was caught up between a child and a young teen. Sometimes she could figure things out well beyond the ability of most adults, and, at other times, it was as if she were a two-year-old. They continued to eat until Griffin's phone went off. Everybody stilled in that instant.

Griffin placed his fork down, picked up his phone, and

checked it. "We're here for the night," he said and placed his phone on the table, then went back to eating.

Lorelei resumed eating too. "But we don't know beyond that?"

"No," he said with a smile, "we don't know beyond that."

"We should know beyond that," Amelia Rose said. "How come you don't know what happens later? Aren't you in charge?"

"Plans are happening, and people are being contacted," Griffin said. "For all you know, they're contacting your dad."

She frowned but still nodded. "My dad's not easy to get a hold of."

"Except for the red phone," Lorelei mentioned.

Griffin immediately turned toward her. "What red phone?"

"It's the phone that my dad only takes those calls directly," Amelia Rose said. "It's the one that he knows I can contact him on and not have to go through all his secretaries."

"That's a good phone number to have," he said as he stared at her. "Do you know what that number is?"

She rattled off the number before anybody had a chance to consider whether she should or not. "Don't worry. Poppy told me to only give that number to people I trust. So it's okay that I gave it to you."

Griffin immediately asked, "Did your kidnappers ask for that number or any number for your father or mother?"

"No." Amelia Rose shook her head, then smiled.

Griffin turned to Lorelei, a really worried look on his face.

She frowned. "No. They never asked me or Amelia Rose. … Does that seem odd to you? Or is this normal? Normal for a kidnapping, I mean?"

"Not sure," Griffin said. "But I'm really glad to hear that Amelia Rose knew not to give out this number to the bad men."

Amelia Rose perked up and smiled again.

Jax dialed the number and then handed the phone to Griffin. "It's a safe phone," Jax explained to Lorelei.

When a man answered, Griffin asked, "Gerard?"

"Yes, who is this?" he snapped. "And how did you get this number?"

Griffin immediately put the phone on speaker and looked at Lorelei and Amelia Rose. "Say hi."

Amelia Rose piped up. "Poppy?"

There was silence, then the man on the other phone exploded. "Amelia Rose, is that you, honey?"

"Yes," she said. "We're safe. Griffin and Jax saved us." She gave Poppy a rambling and an almost incoherent explanation of everything they've been through. Finally the father interrupted her gently to make sure that she was not hurt and that she was okay, and then he asked, "Is Lorelei with you?"

"Yes, I'm here too, Gerard." Lorelei's tone was friendly enough but more businesslike. She quickly confirmed what Amelia Rose had been trying to say. "Jax and Griffin are special ops," she said. "We're in a safe house, eating right now."

"Well, thank heavens for that," Gerard snapped. "Let me talk to the men again."

She returned the phone to Griffin. Then she gazed at Amelia Rose, who was now plowing through food but still talking with a bright smile on her face. "See? We're safe now," Amelia Rose said. "And Daddy knows it too."

"Exactly," Lorelei said. "But remember. We're not out of danger. We're still not back in England, and we still have men chasing after us." She tried to keep an ear to the conversation that Griffin was having with Gerard, but it was hard because Amelia Rose kept talking in her other ear. Now that the child had spoken to her father, she was doing much better.

"I understand you were supposed to come to the hotel, sir. Is that plan still happening?"

"No, not now," Gerard said briskly. "I want the two of them back in England immediately."

"Well, we're still in Thailand, but I don't know for how long," Griffin said. "I just need to know if we have more people we need to look after."

"No," Gerard said. "Your orders are to bring her straight home."

"I'll relay that upward," Griffin said formally. And then he hung up and looked at Amelia Rose. "Good thing you could remember that number."

"It's the one thing my poppy made me memorize," she said. "And I didn't forget, did I?" She turned to look at Lorelei. "He can't be mad at you this time."

"I don't think he'll be mad at me for a while," Lorelei said, "although I could be wrong."

"Will he blame you for the kidnapping?" Griffin asked in confusion.

"It's possible," she said. "I was following instructions, but I wasn't expecting to be kidnapped at a hotel."

"And both of you escaped once too, didn't you?"

Lorelei slid a glance toward her charge, but she nodded.

"Yes, but that didn't work out so well in the end, so it's not something that we're worrying about right now."

"It's my fault," Amelia Rose said. "I couldn't run anymore. And they caught us." She grabbed the salad and put more veggies on her plate. "Nobody told me veggies would make me run more."

"Well, now you know," Jax said in a serious tone. "You always need to keep fit, and you always need to eat the proper food. You never know when you'll get into a tough spot and need that energy."

Amelia Rose nodded soberly. "Now that I know, I'll look after myself better."

Lorelei was surprised to hear that. She faced Griffin. "Can you get us out of the country?"

"Do you have any documents with you?"

"No," she said, "everything was stolen when we were kidnapped."

"What about at your hotel? Is any of that material still there?"

"Possibly," she said, "but I don't really want anybody from that location to know that we're still alive."

"Meaning, that they're involved?"

"Or meaning, that they don't need to lose their jobs over us," she said. "And, if they are in trouble, we don't want them to get into more trouble. Not with those men. Not with what they are capable of."

"One of us will return to your hotel," Jax said. "See if any of your stuff is there that we can retrieve."

"I doubt they held the rooms for us," she said.

"How long were you booked for?"

She stopped, stared, and nodded. "That's right. We were booked for seven days."

"So, even if you weren't physically there, they have no reason to take away your room or to store your belongings elsewhere." Griffin glanced at Jax. "I'll go there later to-night."

"Good," Jax said. "I'll stay here on watch."

And that's what they did. As soon as the dishes were done. and the table was cleared off, Griffin stood, snagged his laptop and phone, and he turned to Jax. "I'm taking the bug detector, but I'm leaving the car in case you need to move quickly. I'll pick up a ride for me. Track me via my phone."

"I'm on it," Jax said it.

Then Lorelei watched Griffin walk out the door.

GRIFFIN ARRIVED IN his stolen vehicle and parked it five zigzagged blocks away, near a commercial district, so, even if the kidnappers tracked him to this car, they would have no idea which business he went into. Yet, if the kidnappers had any brains, they'd know he was too close to this hotel not to be coming here. So Griffin would make this a fast trip in and out.

He approached the hotel with a nonchalance that he was far from feeling. He'd already done a quick check around the perimeter, careful to avoid any cameras. And found neither security nor armed guards. Nobody had shown any signs of extra force. He walked inside with another group, choosing one with a couple tall guys that he could effectively hide behind while facing away from any cameras in the lobby, casually watching the elevators and jumping on with another group of tall visitors, and headed up to the rooms that

Lorelei had told him they had for themselves. Amelia Rose's father was supposed to get the room across from them. It was an interesting choice. They could have had a family suite that would have been a little grander. But maybe the father planned to switch it when he got here. Or he wanted privacy for a female guest traveling with him.

Griffin still wanted confirmation that the father was supposed to come, not just because the father said so. He sent a quick text to Jax to ask the chat window people.

On it.

Because, if the father was involved in something like this, Griffin needed a little more proof of what was going on. And it didn't make any sense that the father would be involved, but Griffin didn't want to exclude anybody at this point. That way just led to problems.

Once upstairs, other people stepped off the elevator with him, and the only camera on the floor seemed to be here, so it captured his back at best. Standing at the hotel room door, he stopped, double-checked the room number, and then quickly unlocked it with his tools. He stepped inside; the bedroom appeared to be just as the women had left it. Their clothes were here; their suitcases were here; everything they needed was here. And more—Nurse's belongings too.

He quickly searched for cameras. Found none. He gave the bug detector a good sweep over the rooms. Again nothing. At least that was good. He surveyed the rooms again, reminding himself to get in and to get out fast.

He frowned, thought about it, and decided he might as well take what he could with him. He quickly packed everything up in the first bedroom, then went through to the second bedroom and found the same thing. Only here, Amelia Rose and all her clothes had been unpacked neatly and placed in the dresser. He quickly packed it all back up and then did a sort through to make sure that all the beddings and clothes were clean of listening devices or cameras, just to make sure the bug detector didn't miss anything.

He found no messages left here by the girls or the kidnappers as far as Griffin could tell. He found no cell phones. The kidnapper had at least taken them. Yet Griffin found a couple laptops as he packed up their belongings.

He knew that the girls were a little suspicious of everyone else still, and rightfully so, but as long as he could get their gear to them, that would help them feel like they were a little bit safer.

His phone beeped. A text from Jax.

Earlier airline reservations for father confirmed, then canceled after we were alerted of kidnapping event.

Well, it didn't exonerate Gerard. Maybe he was just good at covering his bases. But it seemed to substantiate his statement.

With four suitcases now making his exit a little bit more awkward, Griffin stepped out of the hotel room and wheeled the two big ones, with the other two thrown over each shoulder, while heading toward the service elevator, where thankfully there were no cameras. He stepped inside and let it take him down to the very bottom, which was the service garage, where he'd have more choices as to which vehicle to steal this time.

Once inside the dim, gloomy area, he found a dark corner, moved the luggage off to the side, and quickly chose his ride. He had just unlocked the passenger side when a vehicle entered the underground parking area on the far side. He quietly loaded up his new vehicle with the girls' stuff, and, as he hopped into the driver's side, he watched as four men got out of a van, carrying weapons.

They had his undivided attention now.

They walked over to the door that led directly into the hotel and stood on either side, as if standing guard. He frowned, but then another vehicle showed up with two more men inside. One man hopped out and walked toward the other four, shouting in a rapid-fire way.

Using his camera, Griffin took photos of the man approaching the hotel and of the four gunmen. When somebody glanced in his direction, Griffin turned his head, as he started up the engine and slowly drove past. When he came near the two vehicles that they had driven, he took several photos, including the license plates, but couldn't get decent shots of the driver, still in the second vehicle. He got several but doubted they'd lead to any facial match. He drove past them, up and out onto the street. He parked around the corner, locked up the vehicle, and rushed back into the garage. There he could see the four armed men standing around the vehicles and discussing something. So the head guy and the driver with him must have entered the hotel, as there was no sign of those two.

Frowning, Griffin sent the photos to Jax, asking him to look up these men. And then Griffin headed to the side of the van so he could hear their conversation. Some words were in English, and some were not. It was a guttural mix of both. But from what he understood, the boss man got immediate word from a hotel staff member that the suite of rooms had been cleaned out.

His heart sank that his visit had been discovered so quickly. Obviously this was a trap to get another chance at kidnapping the girls. Well, at least that part of the kidnappers' plan didn't happen. But the last thing Griffin wanted to do was throw any extra eyes in their direction. He needed to get the girls away from this whole area, not bring up more questions. Knowing that these armed men were still looking for the girls, and now him, he headed out of the garage but had every intention of entering Lorelei's hotel via the front door.

When his phone buzzed in his pocket, he quickly ducked between two other vehicles and pulled out his cell. And the message came back from Jax saying that the person photographed going into the hotel was the same one who had originally kidnapped the girls. He was the organizer behind it all, as far as Lorelei could tell. License plates were stolen from different vehicles. So no leads there.

Griffin walked up the front steps and through the lobby. It was evening, and a few people wandered around, but mostly the lobby sported muted lighting and a more relaxed and romantic atmosphere as only a hotel could offer. Griffin saw no sign of the man he was looking for.

As Griffin sat in the shadows of the lobby and watched, the elevator opened up, and the same man that he had photographed earlier came walking forward, sending rapid-fire questions at the staff at the front desk. From the bewildered look on their faces, they didn't have a clue what he was talking about. Still, the man kept pointing to the elevator, and then he switched to English and said, "All their stuff is gone. Where did you put it?"

They looked from one to the other and said, "We didn't touch it. Nobody's touched the room as per your orders. All of it was left exactly the same, as you told us to. Nobody's been allowed in."

The kidnapper was obviously well-respected and came with a lot of power.

"Well, somebody not only got in," he said, "but everything's been cleaned out too." He turned, firing off orders to anybody who would listen. "You go and find out now," he roared. "Check the cameras, check everywhere. I want to know who took their luggage."

With everybody focused on the man clearly in charge, Griffin slowly rose to his feet and casually walked out and around the side of the hotel to his new vehicle. There, he hopped into the driver's seat and turned on the engine, and drove slowly back to the apartment. Interesting. They were after all of the girls' possessions now. Why hadn't they taken them in the first place? And why did they want them now?

Unless they planned to recapture the girls—and soon.

CHAPTER 7

LORELEI, ALTHOUGH GRATEFUL to have her belongings back, was more than a little worried with Griffin and Jax in the corner, busy, heads bent together, whispering hard and fast. Griffin showed Jax some photos, and both men then separated, sat down at their laptops, and pounded the keys furiously. She crossed her arms, waited for the right time, and then asked, "So what's happening?"

Griffin didn't even look up. He kept pounding away.

She walked over to him, reached out a hand, and touched him on the shoulder. When he didn't respond, she dug her nails into the cords alongside his neck and said, "Don't ignore me."

He dropped his hands from the keyboard and glared up at her. "Just because I choose not to answer doesn't mean I'm ignoring you."

She raised an eyebrow. "You're not answering me."

"You don't have a question that I can answer."

She brought a chair up and around so she could sit beside him. "Meaning, you don't know what's going on, or you don't want to tell me?"

Jax laughed. "Both."

"And that's not good enough. I've been to hell and back, and I'm very concerned about Amelia Rose. So somebody should start talking."

Griffin, instead, picked up his phone, swiped through, and brought up several photos. "Do you know this man?"

She nodded slowly. "We saw him at the very beginning, but I don't know who he is."

"I do," Jax said. "He's security for a big arms dealer in Thailand. His boss owns the compound you were held at. He's got business deals with governments on a global scale."

"What's that got to do with Gerard's businesses? He's in media."

"I'd say," Griffin added, "that your kidnapper was more into military privatization than anything."

"So that sounds like a rebel, a vigilante, a guerrilla, not an enemy of Gerard's."

"Probably an enemy. Most likely a competitor. Or possibly hired for this job. But then who in Gerard's company would know this guy?"

"Gerard and his sons all deal with international business deals. But you're wasting your time there," she snapped. "Gerard's not into military stuff."

Griffin gave her a flat stare. "How would you know?"

She blinked in confusion, then shook her head. In a low voice, she said, "He's not that kind of guy."

"Yes, he is," Griffin said in a low tone. "The media is a major part of his business, but he's involved in a lot of military contracts for communications as well."

At that, Lorelei sat back and stared at him, stunned. Then she muttered, "I never even considered something like that. But I should have. Communications is a big business, and who needs it the most? Well, *the military*."

"Exactly. And, quite often, communications companies supply their tech—whether software or hardware—for other countries as well."

"So, this guy didn't like the price of Gerard's services?"

"Or Gerard wouldn't do business with him is another possibility. So who would know who he does business with and who he doesn't?" Griffin asked. She winced. "Does any of that sound familiar?"

"I have no clue," she said. "I have nothing to do with his business, and, no, I haven't overheard any conversations about military communications for sure. My job is Amelia Rose."

"Sure," Jax said, "but you're an intelligent woman. You must have gotten some impression as to what's going on."

"But not about this," she protested. "Gerard has had lots of business meetings in his home, but we're always off in a different wing."

"Have you seen many different nationalities come through the house?"

She nodded slowly. "Sure, but I couldn't tell you which ones they were."

"Makes sense," Jax said. "I hate to say it, but Gerard could be dealing with both sides of a war at the same time."

"I couldn't tell you who these people were, not their names," she said, "and all the black limos look the same. I never really saw anybody get out of them. The limos drive in, and they drive out. I don't know who was inside those limos." She motioned at his phone. "Why aren't you sending that photo to Gerard and asking him?"

"I am," he said, "but I've gotten a little more devious, and I'm checking the cameras at the house." He pointed to the monitor in front of her, and she gasped to realize it was the front door of Gerard's biggest family estate that she and Amelia Rose normally lived at.

"Oh, my gosh, how can you do that?"

"I'm doing it for your sake and for her sake," he said bluntly. "And, no, Gerard would not be happy if he knew." Just then a black limo pulled up in the video.

"See? They all look like that," she said. "I think Gerard owns three or four himself."

The driver hopped out, opened up the door behind him, then walked around, and opened up the other door. Several men in business suits exited the vehicle and walked toward the front steps.

"When was this?" she asked, peering closer.

"Three days ago," he said. "I wasn't sure how far back to go in a video feed, but three days earlier brings up some interesting possibilities."

"But this could be legitimate business," she said. "It doesn't mean it has anything to do with our kidnapping."

"Maybe not, but it doesn't mean it doesn't either. In order to understand the enemy, we have to understand the people involved."

She stared at him and said, "I really don't like the way your mind thinks."

He turned, flashed her bright white teeth, and said, "Why don't you lie down and rest?"

She glared at him and leaned closer. "Why don't *you* lie down and rest?"

In a surprise move, he stole a kiss and cheerfully said, "Can't. I'm on duty."

Stunned at the shock of his lips against hers and the spark that had flashed between them, she sat back awkwardly. She crossed her arms over her chest as she tried to figure out what to do next. A gentle exit would have been nice, but she'd passed that point. She looked at Jax and caught him grinning. She glared at him, then announced, "It's not funny."

Immediately he wiped the smile off his face, and, in the gravest of voices, he said, "Absolutely not."

She raised both hands in frustration and said, "You two are impossible."

"Hardly," Griffin said. "You should be grateful to us."

"Yeah? What do you want as thanks?" she asked suspiciously.

He looked at her, and she could see the anger in his eyes. "Not that."

"I didn't think so," she said.

"You'd better not think so," he said in a warning note.

She shrugged and whispered, "Everything's topsy-turvy these days." Then she rubbed her temple. "And I'm getting a hell of a headache sorting my way through it."

"Well, you need to remember," he said gently, "that you're not alone anymore."

She thought about that and brightened. "You're right. I'm not. So you should be able to handle it all." She got up to check on Amelia Rose.

He called out as she walked away, "That's what we've been trying to say."

"Oh, and here I thought you're telling the little woman to go lie down and to not worry her pretty little head about it."

When she heard an odd spluttering sound, she turned to see Jax barely containing his mirth as he stared between the two of them. "You know, if we weren't on the job," he'd said, "I'd suggest you guys grab a hotel for a couple nights and work this through your system."

She spun around yet again, her hands on her hips, and glared at him.

Jax shrugged and said, "I'm just saying. There's enough electricity in this room to crack and cook an egg. If you guys ever let loose that firepower, you two would burn up the sheets."

"I'm not interested in burning up the sheets," she said stiffly.

"I am," Griffin said immediately. "So, if you ever change your mind, let me know."

She gasped out loud and then realized he was teasing, looking at her with the most innocent of looks on his face, but his eyes twinkled. She stormed over and pointed her finger in his face.

"Careful," he whispered in a low tone.

"No, you be careful. Amelia Rose could hear you."

Griffin's gaze hardened. "You should know better than that. I wouldn't tease you like this in front of the child. And you really don't want to get me mad on this subject."

But instead of backing down, she shoved her face against his and said, "Why?"

He grabbed her on either side of her face, tucked her just a little bit closer, and kissed her hard. And, damn, if the passion didn't arise once again, and sparks flashed all around them. She groaned softly, and he forcibly pushed her away and said, "Jax is right. We'd better watch what we're doing."

She shook her head. "What the hell is this?"

"Adrenaline," he said. "Fear, gratitude, danger. It mixes hormones and passion all together. Now leave. Keep temptation away from me, woman."

She snorted. "No problem." And she stormed off to visit Amelia Rose.

IT WAS ALL Griffin could do to stop the laughter from bubbling up and outward. She'd look shocked, frustrated, and frustrated in another way too. He could relate. He shifted back to his laptop and tried to refocus. He knew that Jax was grinning like a crazy man. Griffin just shook his head at him. "Don't say anything."

"I don't have to say anything, aside from maybe I'm the one who'll have to go for a walk and leave you two alone."

"Not with the kid," he muttered.

"Good point," Jax said. "Maybe the kid and I will go for a walk then. For just the briefest of moments."

Griffin considered what that opportunity could mean, and then he shook his head. "Not going to happen. Not while we're on the job. And definitely need longer than *the briefest of moments*."

"You may have to make do," Jax said, "because, when the job's over, there's a good chance you two will be on opposite ends of the earth."

"True." He sighed, his shoulders sagging as he thought about it. But he wasn't a randy teenager anymore, and keeping his own sexual passion in check was something he was used to. He'd sent the photos to his team and had asked them to forward those to Amelia Rose's father. Within minutes, his phone rang. He looked at it. *Gerard*. He quickly answered, putting it on speaker. Jax moved closer.

"So you do recognize that first picture we sent you?" Griffin asked.

"Yes," he said in a harsh tone. "He's one of the men who threatened me if I didn't do business with them. I was supplying China and South Korea with special communications, and they wanted the same deal."

"And you didn't give it to them, I presume?"

"No," Gerard snapped. "I didn't like anything about the deal. And I didn't like anything about the people behind the deal."

"With good reason, it's one of the reasons I went back to the hotel and retrieved their personal belongings," Griffin said. "But now we've got a problem because I think they were behind the kidnapping."

"You went back to the hotel and got their stuff?" Gerard asked curiously. "I don't understand why."

"Because I didn't want to leave anything behind," he said honestly. "It's much better to remove it and not leave bits and pieces the kidnappers can come back for, using them as signs of proof of kidnapping, by sending you a jacket or a skirt or something worse."

"I never thought of that," Amelia Rose's father said. "That's a little disturbing."

"I also wanted to see if somebody at the hotel had been ordered to clean out their rooms. Instead, the staff had been ordered by that man to leave everything left behind as it was."

"They were held in their rooms originally and then moved," Gerard said.

"And how do you know that?" Griffin asked curiously.

"Because the staff said that they couldn't raise anybody in the room, but the doors were all locked, and they were told to stay away. But then, when they went back again for housekeeping, the rooms were empty."

"Likely when they tried to escape out on the beach," Griffin said, his tone low. "Your daughter's feeling very guilty for not keeping up with Lorelei as they ran away."

"She's never been very physically active," her father said with a sigh.

"Well, the good news is, she's at least eating vegetables now," Griffin said drily.

Gerard gave a short bark of laughter. "Well, that's something. She's pure and innocent," he said, soft and gentle. "And I want to make sure she stays that way."

"Until when?" Griffin asked. "You know that she'll grow up at one point in time. This alone has helped her to grow up a lot more. You do realize that she saw Nurse killed in front of her, right?"

There was silence on the other end of the phone, and then Gerard swore deep and heavy. "My poor baby," he whispered finally.

"Nurse's death was to set an example that the two of them behave and follow orders. Nurse was also grabbed and held in the hotel room, the same room that they were in."

"Yes, they had a suite," he said. "I always do that."

"Same suite as for you?"

"No, I reserved my suite across the hall. But it's not like we've traveled to Thailand annually or even every few years, and we don't stay at the same hotel regardless," he said, his voice distant. "The girls must have been seen at the reception desk or on their way back and forth to the hotel."

"Time to get them fake IDs then when they travel, to register them at hotels under those fake names too."

"Maybe … if she ever travels again. I understand the microchip helped you to identify where they were?"

"Yes. They were being held in a compound owned by that well-known arms dealer the kidnapper works for," Griffin confirmed. "But the girls were then moved that night, and we caught up with them when the kidnapper's vehicle was sidelined by an accident."

"Did you cause the accident?"

Griffin gave a short laugh. "No, not this time. Otherwise the chase would have gone on much longer. As it was, there was a big pileup, and it was a pretty ugly crash site. The kidnappers were at the head of the line. I came up behind, managed to get the girls, and we turned around and got out of there, while more cars drove up and boxed in the kidnappers."

"Well, I'm grateful for that," he said. "Have you any idea who else might be involved?"

"No. We're still running background checks on everybody in your company and your family, especially anyone who would know the arms dealer," Griffin said smoothly. Then he waited. And Gerard didn't disappoint.

"My company and my family?" he roared.

"Yes," Griffin said. "It could be that this is a complete blackmail scheme from the outside, perhaps orchestrated by your denied military man. But somebody had to know your schedule pretty well. Somebody had to understand that the three females would be completely alone on this trip. This wasn't just by chance that they got kidnapped. No 'Oh, look. There are three people we can kidnap and run a ransom deal through.'"

"The way you put it," Gerard said, "I guess that makes sense. But I run heavy security checks on everybody in my company. Nobody would dare cross me."

"And that just means that somebody already has," Griffin said with a heavy sigh. "Look. I know that you run communications and consider yourself high-tech. Often though, shit like this is very close to home."

"How close?" Gerard asked, but his voice held a warning, as if Griffin wasn't to cross the line.

"Well, if you don't think that I'll check in on your sons

and your wife, you're wrong," Griffin said coolly. "Because this kidnapping event won't happen again. That little girl's been through enough shit. And Nurse did not deserve to be murdered on a holiday a long way away from home."

"No, she didn't even want to go," Gerard groaned. "My wife insisted."

"And I understand that your wife and your daughter don't have a close relationship."

There was silence on the other end. "That's quite true, but that doesn't mean Wendy would do anything to harm Amelia Rose," he said briskly, almost dismissing the concept out of hand.

"And, for that, I need to understand how the inheritance works, upon your death." Griffin knew he was crossing some major personal lines here. "A lot of people would benefit if your daughter doesn't survive either."

"There's enough money to go around," he snapped. "And I don't want you making accusations against my family."

"Outside of your sons and your wife, who else stands to inherit?"

"My brother and his family," he said. "My brother's been my vice president for a good twenty years."

"And do they all get a big-enough piece of the pie that they're all happy?"

"They should be," he said. "They get a decent voting block now, but that doesn't change much with my death."

"And how do your sons feel about that?"

"They are fine with it," he said, his tone turning bewildered. "You don't really think somebody is angling for more, do you?"

"The problem with being greedy," Griffin said, "is that

generally you're too greedy to see where enough is enough." On that note, he changed tact and said, "I need the name of your brother and the names of the family members that work for you."

Gerard gave him the list and then said, "You better be wrong about this."

"I hope I am," Griffin said. "But, so far, somebody has already kidnapped your daughter, twice, and killed your nurse. I'm sure you feel that something needs to be done after Amelia Rose has been put through so much."

"Well, as soon as I get my daughter and Lorelei home, Lorelei will get a raise. And Amelia Rose may never leave the country again."

"And that would make sense," Griffin said, "but it's not necessarily the right answer."

"So, what are you thinking?"

"I'm wondering why you didn't send any security with the women, traveling to a foreign country." Griffin stared down at the phone, waiting to hear what response Gerard would give.

In a slow tone, he said, "That was my wife's idea. She felt that traveling with security was stifling. She never did see that there was any danger."

But even Griffin could hear the broken tone in the man's voice. "I know about your first son," Griffin said. "And I'm sorry about that. I guess that's partly why it surprised me that the women were traveling alone."

"Because I got complacent," he said, his voice returning, vibrating with anger. "Something I won't forget again."

"And whose idea was it that the three women travel here on their own?"

"My wife's," he said, "but I agreed."

"And how often does something like this happen?"

Silence. "Not very often. Usually my wife or I travel with them."

"So, when was the one last time that the two women traveled alone with Amelia Rose?"

"I'm not sure they ever have," he said, his voice rising.

"And you still haven't received a blackmail notice?"

"No, I was expecting it anytime now. I was taken with my firstborn son a long time ago, but he was only two years old, and they separated him from me. The kidnappers blackmailed my father, who started this company and was doing quite well at the time. Nothing like it is now, mind you, but enough that the kidnappers figured to cash in on his success. They made him and me sit and sweat and panic for three or four days, and *then* they sent a note with a ransom demand. Immediately he jumped on it and tried to pay"— his tone turned harsh, unforgiving—"but …"

"And then you were betrayed?"

"Yes, I was betrayed," he agreed. "The money was picked up. I was released at the gate of the estate, still tied up and a hood over my head, and my son's dead body was dumped close by. The cops never found the killers," he said, the old grief still catching his tone.

"So, you assumed that it would be a similar scenario this time?"

"Yes. Only I don't understand this game. Yes, I was expecting a ransom note. Thank God, you have them safe. I need to know what the play is here. I don't understand, but I can't lose another child this way."

"No," Griffin said. "I don't understand either. At least not yet."

CHAPTER 8

L ORELEI HAD SPENT some time calming Amelia Rose, especially after hearing her poppy's raised voice on the phone. The child was soon placated, but she clung to Lorelei. Both girls had moved to the couch in the living room of the apartment, where Amelia Rose soon fell asleep and where Lorelei fidgeted, near enough to hear the conversation on speaker still ongoing in the kitchen.

When the call ended, Griffin leaned back in his chair, his face thoughtful and pensive, she hopped to her feet and ran toward him. She didn't even question when he opened his arms, and she threw herself into them to give him a hug. "You don't look so good."

"I'm fine," he said. He frowned and noted that Amelia Rose was once again lying down. "Is she sleeping? Through all that yelling?"

Lorelei nodded. "She's been sleeping a lot lately. I think she sleeps to avoid thinking about the emotional scenarios, like her poppy on the phone just now."

"Stress will do that to you as well," he said. He glanced at Jax, hunkered over his laptop at the kitchen table. Griffin swept his arm in that direction. Lorelei sank into a chair next to Jax, Griffin joining them, and all three of their heads bent together as they spoke in low tones.

"Do you have a suspect?" she whispered. "A business

enemy or family?"

"I'm not sure," Griffin said, "but let's look at this. The brothers gain Amelia Rose's interest in the estate if their sister doesn't get home. Her uncle gains as well if she doesn't get home. And the wife, what would she gain?"

"Depends if she's setting up the blackmail," Jax stated. "Imagine if she gets, say, a ten-million-dollar ransom. She ends up with her daughter and gains the money and is free of Gerard, free to live elsewhere, to remain separated informally if not legally. Plus, like any blackmail, she's free to blackmail Gerard again if Wendy maintains possession of Amelia Rose. It's the ultimate ATM."

"Meaning that, there's a prenup, where she doesn't get very much and can't stand staying with him and wants a new way to start a new life but with tons of money?" she interpreted Jax's comment.

Both men looked at her in surprise but then nodded. "Exactly."

"That's a bit rough," she said. "But honestly, I could see her having her own daughter kidnapped. She's not family oriented but is all about Gerard's money and the house and living the high life."

"Can you give us an example of what you mean?"

Her voice lowered as she leaned closer. "Gerard is no saint but tries to keep his affairs quiet, but she's makes no attempt to be discreet—jumps all men between fifteen and fifty, anywhere and anytime, even if Amelia Rose is around. Drinks like a fish and shows no loyalty to her husband at home or out in public. I know he's sick of her, but I don't know if he's done anything about a divorce yet. Honestly, I can't believe he's put up with her antics this long, even if she is Amelia Rose's mother."

"And that sucks," Griffin said. "It's bad enough to think that you've been kidnapped because of your father's business dealings, but do you really want to hear that all this terror you were put through was because of your mother's machinations?"

"What about Nurse?" Jax asked. "What was the relationship between Amelia Rose's mother and Nurse?"

Lorelei winced. "The worst," she said slowly. "Wendy wanted Mary fired. Said Nurse was old and useless."

The two men exchanged hard glances.

She shrugged, then frowned. "But to go from wanting Nurse fired to then arranging for the woman to be killed, … that's pretty cold, even for Wendy."

"Depends on what ransom money might have come through."

"But they didn't have to kill Nurse for that," she protested. "She could have been rescued, and the mother still gets her money. Then she leaves behind Gerard and Nurse. Maybe even Amelia Rose. Oh my …"

"Surely Wendy or whoever won't even try for a ransom now that Gerard knows his daughter has been rescued, or is another party in play?" Jax asked.

Just then a text message came from Gerard. **Ransom note just came through. Twenty-five million. Unmarked bills tomorrow night at a specified location. Please confirm you still have my daughter.**

Instead of responding by text, Griffin hit Dial and handed the phone to Lorelei, as she turned to watch Amelia Rose still resting on the couch.

As soon as she heard Gerard's voice, she said, "Gerard, this is Lorelei. We have her. She's sound asleep."

"Oh, thank God," he said, and she could hear the fear

and anxiety threatening his voice. "So, what the hell's going on here?"

"I'm putting you on speaker," she said, and she hit the button and laid the phone on the table.

"I highly suspect," Griffin said, "we have kidnappers who lost their bait but will try to get the ransom money anyway. While they still look to recapture your little girl, they'll see if they can get a money drop and run."

"So they're assuming then that you guys have gone to ground and haven't contacted me. Is that it?"

"Well, if it wasn't for your daughter remembering the number of your red phone," Griffin said, "the normal route would be to take the little girl to the police, right?"

"Or at least a consulate, yes," he said.

"In which case, the media would have already found out."

"Particularly given our names," he affirmed. "So, … because the media hasn't told the story, you're thinking that the kidnappers don't know who has my daughter and Lorelai or if their two victims escaped on their own or if somebody even worse has them. And, while they track down the location of their victims, they'll still stick to the plan."

"Wouldn't you?" Jax challenged.

Gerard sighed. "Of course. Anybody would. So I still have to show up at that meet."

"Get MI6 assistance and set it up so you snag whoever is picking up the money. That event is set to happen on English soil, so MI6 would want to take part in this."

"They are already involved," Gerard said.

"Good. And hopefully, with any luck, we'll snag whoever is behind it on your end. We're still on the lookout here for the kidnappers to make another move on the girls, but just know that, at the moment, we're all safe."

"Good," Gerard said, his voice stronger. "Lorelei, you still there?"

"Yes, Gerard, I'm here."

"I just wanted to say," he said, his voice choked up, "I wanted to say, *thank you*. Thanks for keeping Amelia Rose safe."

She smiled. "I said I would. It's been a pretty rough trip so far. So, the next time you plan a holiday, may I suggest we pick the South of France?"

He gave a burst of shallow laughter and said, "That sounds like a good idea to me. And I will ask that you keep looking after her the same way as you have been. I don't think I could stand to lose another child."

"We have no intention of letting that happen," Griffin said.

"Good," Gerard said. "Losing one was horrific. The thought of losing another one? ... No, I'd rather shoot myself first."

After that conversation ended, Lorelei decided it was time to call it a night. This had been one long ugly Tuesday. She went to bed early after Jax moved Amelia Rose from the couch to a proper bed, hoping that maybe she and Lorelei could finally get a decent night's sleep. They were obviously still in danger, hiding from whoever was after them locally, but there had been an amazing amount of progress. She knew the men were staying up for a while, sorting through the information.

It was all a bit confusing for her because she was more about teaching her charge instead of studying new people close up. She knew Gerard considered himself a great judge of human character, but he'd married Wendy, so how good a judge could he be? Not to mention the fact that they were still married and that confused Lorelei. Unless it was only for Amelia Rose's sake, in which case the marriage would be done relatively soon or at least in seven years when Amelia Rose became an adult. To think though, that the mother might have had a hand in her daughter's abduction was beyond Lorelei's comprehension.

No, she refused to believe it until there was proof.

Amelia Rose was a gorgeous little girl inside and out, and she was just on the brink of entering young womanhood. Lorelei knew Amelia Rose would take the world by storm in whatever direction she chose. But more than that, Lorelei had been privileged to be a part of Amelia Rose's journey so far. At one point in time, Lorelei wanted children of her own, so tutoring Amelia Rose had been an interesting trial. Lorelei laughed at that word because there hadn't been very much in the way of trials with the child. So maybe it wasn't a good test after all for having a child of her own.

And, of course, she'd started on the job when Amelia Rose was already six, so Lorelei had missed her early years. Amelia Rose adored spending time with her poppy but not so much for time spent with her mother. In that way, Amelia Rose instinctively understood the difference between quality time versus just putting in time. Lorelei could easily see the reason why.

Still, it was late. Better she stop this endless mental loop and get some sleep.

Lorelei had her suitcase now, giving her clean PJs for tonight and fresh clothes for tomorrow. She quickly had a shower, taking extra long to do her hair, which was dark blonde and looking almost black with dust and dirt. She rinsed and washed it several times and then, when she stepped out, not wanting to go to bed with it all wet, braided it in a thick plait down the center of her back. Finally clean and realizing she could afford to sleep, at least right now, she dressed in her summer pajamas of a camisole and matching boy shorts and crawled into bed.

She was hoping that the monsters would stay away tonight. But she was afraid, as tired as she was, that was almost an invitation to let them in again. And she'd have no control because she'd be asleep, and her subconscious would be running the show. She slowly closed her eyes and drifted off. But it wasn't long before someone chased her and the child, her lungs burning as she tried to carry Amelia Rose along and to help her move faster and faster. Lorelei could feel the panic threatening to choke her. And, when she finally woke up with a cry choking in her throat and her heart pounding desperately to get free of her chest, she sat up in bed and gulped air.

Griffin stood in her bedroom doorway, staring at her.

He took three short steps to her bedside, sat down, and pulled her into his arms.

She burrowed in deep. "Will the nightmares ever stop?"

"Yes," he said, "they will. But maybe not as fast as you'd like them to."

She didn't even want to contemplate his words. But it was understandable. Time helped heal and added distance to a lot of things. She sighed and tried to pull back, but he had nothing to do with it. He just held her close and whispered against her hair, "Relax and remember that you're not alone. We're here to help, and we're here to protect. Your cry was terrifying enough that it almost gave me a heart attack. So I need these few moments."

That gurgled a laugh out of her. She looked up to see his

grin flash. "You said that on purpose," she murmured.

He grinned, nodded, kissed her on the temple, and said, "I did, but you're obviously feeling a little bit better. Now lay back down, and I'll pull the covers over you. If you want, I'll stay in the chair in the room."

"No," she said, "I should be fine." At least she should be inside. She didn't know if she would be or not. But it was ridiculous to think she would need him to stay in the room with her. She curled up under the covers, and he tucked her in and dropped yet a second kiss on her temple, making her wonder at the ease and naturalness of it on both their parts. And then she listened as he walked away. She counted his steps to the doorway and then couldn't do it. "Stop."

He froze, returned to her side, and whispered, "What?"

She groaned. "I don't want you to stay, mentally, because I know I need to handle this," she whispered in frustration. "But just the thought of you leaving right now is making my heart pound, and I can hardly breathe."

Instead of grabbing the chair on the far side, he nudged her over and laid atop the covers beside her. He wrapped an arm around her and pulled her against him. "Sleep," he said. "It's much easier to deal with everything in life if you have rest. When you don't, the problems seem bigger and much harder to find a way around. So, let's sleep tonight and worry about it later."

She hated being weak. She hated knowing the sense of security that just being in his arms gave her. But she wouldn't look a gift horse in the mouth. As long as he insisted, she could acquiesce. She snuggled deeper into the blankets, yawned once, and then whispered, "Thank you."

He gently hugged her closer and whispered, "You're welcome. Now go to sleep."

When she woke yet again a few hours later, arms were wrapped around her and held her close. She twisted and turned until she saw it was once again or maybe still Griffin. She opened her eyes to reassure herself and, seeing his gentle concerned face, closed her eyes and drifted off to sleep again. When she woke yet again, she struggled less, recognizing his touch, and finally fully woke this time. It was early morning, and he snored gently beside her. She smiled and whispered, "I wonder if you got enough sleep."

She checked the time to see it was past seven in the morning. She slipped out of bed, grabbed her clothes, dressed in the bathroom, and then walked away, leaving him to snooze gently on her bed. She stepped out into the main apartment to find Jax up and making coffee.

He looked at her, smiled, and said, "Is he still sleeping?"

Embarrassed, she nodded and whispered, "I don't think he got much sleep though. I kept waking up, screaming."

"To be expected," he said seriously. "And I would have done the same, but he got there before me." He waggled his eyebrows at her.

She chuckled. "Not likely."

"Absolutely," he said. "Not to make this all about the danger right now, but we need you as focused and as capable of running if need be as we can."

She immediately winced, hearing the reason behind his wish to help her. "In theory," she said, "I know that. But, in reality, it sucks to think that's the reason he was in there."

"No," Jax said, "don't misunderstand." He pressed the button for the coffee and turned to face her. "That's the reason either one of us would have gone to settle you, but he didn't have to stay. He did that because he cares."

She could feel the warmth blossoming inside. "Dangerous time to be caring about somebody," she said lightly. "It's likely the danger that's heightening his emotions."

"Maybe for you," he said bluntly. "But this is the work Griffin has done for years. I don't remember a single case where he spent the night holding a woman close just so she didn't have to battle nightmares on her own."

She sagged into the kitchen chair, thinking about that. "He really lives up to his name, doesn't he?" She tried to add a note of humor to it but there was a softness in her voice, and she knew that Jax caught it.

He nodded. "He's always been a protector. And he's been hurt a couple times."

"Haven't we all?" she asked, staring off in the distance. She gave herself a mental shake and said, "While I was battling demons, what kind of night did Amelia Rose have?"

"She slept like a rock," he said. "Unbelievably so."

"She always has had that ability," Lorelei nodded. "I was very jealous of it, even before this trip."

"You don't sleep most of the time?"

"I do," she said, "when I'm in my own bed, but I'm not as comfortable being out and about in the world, so traveling generally impacts my sleeping."

"That's the same for a lot of people," he said. "But at least you're doing fine now."

"I'm definitely doing a lot better, after some sleep," she said. "Not to mention a shower and a clean change of clothes." She motioned at the clothes she had on. "I wonder why they never cleaned out our rooms before?"

"I bet they're regretting it now," he said, "because they obviously lost that advantage. Not to mention the fact that we knew where you weren't."

"Can they track Griffin?"

"I doubt it," Jax said. "He's a shadow in the night."

"But even shadows …" she whispered, trying hard to still panic in her heart, "shadows create shapes."

He nodded seriously, brought cups over to the table, and sat down as they waited for the pot to drip. "But he's very good at what he does. And we won't be here for long anyway."

She looked at him in surprise. "That's too bad," she said. "I was hoping you'd stay."

"No," he said, "we all have passage back to England."

"Interesting," she said with a frown. "How are we traveling?"

He smiled. "Underwater."

She stared at him in shock. "What?"

"We need to get you out of sight of cameras and away from everybody, so our choices were public transport, private transport, or we had to get creative."

She stared at him. "Underwater? Not scuba diving, right?"

"Don't worry about it," he said. "We got this."

She hated to say it because she knew they did have it, but it was still disconcerting. "Does Gerard know?"

Jax shook his head. "Better that nobody knows. We want to make sure there are no leaks and no betrayals anywhere along this process."

"Fine," she said. "I'm all for that. What's the first step of this unique journey we're taking?"

"Some interesting flights," he said with a grin. "You don't get seasickness or motion sickness, do you?"

She shook her head. "No, both Amelia Rose and I are good travelers that way."

"That's good," he said as the coffeemaker beeped. "Because this could be a fun ride."

He got up, poured the coffee, and wouldn't say another word.

GRIFFIN HAD WOKEN up as she left and took a few moments to go to the bathroom, scrub his face, and begin the day. He walked out hearing Jax telling Lorelei about the next step of the journey. Griffin headed for the coffeepot and poured himself a cup. "Have we confirmed all the details yet?"

"Almost," Jax said. "Just the first leg is in question."

"Right," he said, "and that's the most important one."

"I think it's more or less resolved. We're just waiting for a final confirmation."

"Do we have time for food?" Lorelei asked.

"We do," Jax said.

On that note, Griffin walked to the fridge and pulled out eggs and bacon. A little bit of chicken was left, but they had pretty well scoffed up everything else. He brought out those leftovers from the fridge too and said, "This is what we have to work with." He started the eggs and bacon and watched as Lorelei got up and snagged a piece of chicken and stood there by the table, eating it.

"How did you finally sleep?" he asked, his voice low and soft, but that gaze of hers, well, it would melt his heart if she lit it.

She smiled up at him. "Well, at least I slept, thanks to you. You didn't have to spend the whole night, you know?"

"In order for you to get to sleep, yes," he said, "I did."

"Did you get any sleep?" she asked worriedly. "There's

no point in your rescued kidnap victims being safe and able to run if the guy who is protecting them isn't."

Jax laughed beside her. "She's got a point there, Griffin."

"I slept pretty decently," he said, surprised that he felt strong and capable. As soon as the bacon was perfectly cooked, he laid it on a paper towel and mixed up the rest of the eggs into a scramble. With the last of the bread, he made toast and said, "Food's a bit of a mix-up, but it's what we've got."

Just then a sound came from the other bedroom. Lorelei bolted to her feet and raced in. Both men froze as they listened to the girls' conversation. Then realizing that the child's cry was followed by laughter, they both calmed down.

Jax looked over at Griffin. "You're getting in too deep."

Griffin stopped stirring the scrambled eggs in the pan. He looked over at his friend and said, "Maybe."

"Did you think about that?"

"No," he said, "I didn't. Not sure I can either."

"Meaning?"

"I think it's already too late. I've met a lot of women in my time, but I can't say too many have affected me like this."

"Just stay objective," Jax said.

"I will be," he said. "I have to admit that I'm operating under a new set of parameters. I've never had anybody I cared about to this extent."

"I know," Jax said. "I guess that's why I'm bringing it up. We want to make sure that decisions are still made for the right reasons."

"I'm always a pro. You know that," he said. He turned off the burner and quickly dished up the scrambled eggs into a serving bowl, then he called out, "Lorelei and Amelia Rose, breakfast."

He finished setting the table, holding off looking in the girls' direction as they came toward him because he knew, like Jax had seen, Griffin's gaze would go first to Lorelei, if only for the chance to see her again. And how sad was that? He lifted his gaze to see her warm brown eyes staring at him and a grin at the corner of her lips.

"She slept well," Lorelei announced. "She says two heroes are looking after us, so there's no reason for her to have any nightmares."

Amelia Rose bounced forward and threw her arms around Griffin and gave him a big hug. Then she walked over to the table where Jax sat and hugged him from behind. Jax chuckled, turned around, picked her up, and stood with her in his arms, then tossed her once. She let out a shriek.

Lorelei looked at him in amazement. "How can you even lift her?" she asked enviously. "I don't have that kind of strength."

"You don't need it either," Griffin said as he motioned at the table. "Sit down. Let's get eating."

Obediently she sat on the chair beside him, just like how he would have sat beside her. They were almost like homing pigeons, instinctively seeking each other out in the darkness. And he knew just how bad he really did have it. Amelia Rose, on the other hand, was more than happy to sit beside Jax, even pulling her chair closer toward him.

"Did you get any sleep, Jax?" She chattered away as she dug in, scooping up eggs with a serving spoon but then snagging up bacon with her fingers. Lorelei immediately chided her for her fingers, but she just grinned up at her. "Jax uses his fingers," she said.

And Jax deliberately reached across, used his fingers, and

snagged more bacon.

Lorelei groaned. "You two are incorrigible."

But Griffin, not to be outdone, using his fingers, chose two pieces for himself but also two for her and dropped those in her plate. He raised an eyebrow and said, "One does what one must …"

She gave him a special smile that hit him hard. He dropped his gaze to his plate, confused, irritated, and frustrated at the timing. When he raised his gaze again, Jax looked at him with a warning in his gaze. Griffin gave a brief nod and tucked into his food. Objectivity was everything in this game.

And, in games like this, making a mistake was fatal.

CHAPTER 9

SOMETHING HAD DEFINITELY changed between her and Griffin. Lorelei wanted to spend time in a corner with a cup of tea and really delve into what was going on, but there was no time. As soon as they finished eating, the men had bounced up, cleaned up the kitchen, and packed up the rest of food into a large Ziploc bag, which she didn't quite understand, until she realized that it was all leaving with them. She raced back to her room, quickly made the bed, and checked that there were no obvious signs of anybody having been here. Then she went to Amelia Rose's room and did the same.

With the bags packed and sitting at the front door, Griffin made a final tour through the apartment and opened the front door that led to the hallway. Jax was out first, checking that the coast was clear. And then he nodded toward Griffin. Jax grabbed half their luggage and had his duffel on his back and motioned for Lorelei and Amelia Rose to follow Griffin, who carried the rest of their luggage. He headed forward and hit the button on the elevator, Jax behind them all. As soon as they all stepped in, instead of going down, they went up.

Lorelei's eyebrows went up too. She frowned at him, but Griffin gave a small shake of his head, and she understood it wasn't the time to ask questions. This was the time to go with the flow if she wanted to get her and Amelia Rose out of here safely. With her heart hammering against her ribs, she hung on to Amelia Rose, not giving the girl a chance to back away from her.

Amelia Rose looked at her and whispered, "It'll be okay, Lorelei."

She was probably hurting the child's hand with her panicked grip, so she gentled her hold. Lorelei gave a small chuckle and said, "I hope so."

"It's all good," Amelia Rose said. "These guys will look after us just fine." And her tone was so confident that Lorelei was amazed. Was that the innocence of a child who hadn't seen quite enough of the world to understand just how ugly the underbelly could be? Yet she'd seen Nurse killed. So maybe it was about trusting in *these* heroes.

When they got to the floor they wanted, after they had bypassed all the others, Jax quickly moved to another elevator and motioned them inside. Without question, the four piled in with all their luggage, and he hit another button. When the elevator doors opened this time, they found a small entranceway with glass doors in front.

They were on the roof.

Lorelei gasped as Griffin opened the glass door and stepped outside, getting them to move quickly. Apparently they were on a schedule. They followed her out, and she would have asked a question but couldn't be heard as a helicopter flew overhead and suddenly landed in front of them. She looked at Griffin, and he nodded, grabbed her arm, and said in a low voice against her ear, "Hang on to Amelia Rose."

Jax was already ahead of them. He spoke with the pilot and opened the back door, tossing up luggage. He called over to them, "Come on."

They quickly raced forward, with Griffin showing them how to duck below the rotors. Then he picked up Lorelei and lifted her into the chopper and did the same with Amelia Rose. Jax stowed their luggage safely, belting it in. Once inside, both men climbed up, and they went to town, locking down harnesses on both girls. They took seats across from them, even while the pilot lifted the helicopter. The doors were off, and she got a bird's-eye view of the city as they soared high above.

The pilot flew for about forty minutes and then landed at what looked like a yacht club. He set the helicopter down, and, without another word, the men got off, helping the girls and taking the luggage with them. There, they strode toward the end of a single long dock. They moved quickly and efficiently, not running, but Lorelei and Amelia Rose had to run to keep up. Lorelei was afraid that that in itself would cause attention. But, when she got to the end, a speedboat, and a big one at that, sat nearby.

Surprised—yet nothing really surprised her anymore— she hopped in, accepted the life jackets that they were both given, put hers on, and then helped buckling up Amelia Rose. The girl was well on her way to getting it buckled herself when they were off again.

Lorelei had no clue where they were going, but apparently it was important that they get there fast. The speedboat was noisy, too noisy to talk and be heard. The wind was brutal too. Even behind the windshield, it wasn't enough to stop the cold wind from biting each of them. Even though the temperature and the sun were hot, that wind-shear factor was something else. But they came up against another large yacht and were quickly disembarked onto the new vessel. Finally, when the speedboat left, she turned and looked up at

Griffin. "I get the need for speed but that thing is dangerous to anybody's hearing."

He nodded but didn't say a word about the remark but instead said, "Now we'll stay here on deck for another short trip."

She smiled at him while he pulled out a laptop. She saw he had a satellite feed link that appeared to be directly overhead. "Is that us?"

"Now we wait," he said with a nod.

She smiled and nodded, but the yacht was quite a ways offshore. She didn't have a clue where they would go. That speedboat had taken a tremendous amount of energy from her. They'd been on it for just long enough for her to completely lose her orientation. She sat down with Amelia Rose beside her.

"How long are we waiting?" Amelia Rose asked.

"A while."

Amelia Rose piped up and asked more questions. She wanted to know how big the yacht was, how fast it could go, whose it was, and could they go to one of the rooms on it. Jax answered each and every one of her questions patiently and calmly, with as much information as he could.

And, for the last part, he said, "No, you can't."

She looked up at him and pouted. "My dad has a yacht," she announced.

"I'm sure he does," Jax said with a smile. "But this is one of those mega-yachts. I doubt his is this big, although it could be."

She shrugged. "I never get to go on it. Maybe it's bigger?"

"Maybe that's what we should do next time," Lorelei said. "Maybe you can get your dad to go on the yacht with us."

"Maybe," she said doubtfully. "I think he leases it."

Lorelei didn't know how long they would wait. It seemed like they were expecting another ride immediately, but that didn't happen, and the yacht stormed ahead at a decent rate. She frowned, but, when wondering if they would get a cup of coffee or at least some water, a trolley was pushed down to the far corner.

Jax retrieved it and brought it forward. "Oh, nice, anything anybody could want," he announced. And, sure enough, there was a pot of tea and a pot of coffee, sandwiches, and little extras, like cheese and fruit. She grabbed two plates, took a selection, passing one plate to Amelia Rose and sat back down where she had been, so she could stare out at the ocean. And to sit close to Griffin.

"I have no idea how you made all this happen," she said, "but thank you."

"It's what we do," Griffin said.

"Well, maybe," she said, "but I wonder just how much you do versus how much your team does."

"True enough," he said with a chuckle. "You don't do any of this without a team behind you."

She nodded. "Not to mention money."

"Most people aren't paid for their part in this," he said.

In light of their kidnapping for a multimillion-dollar ransom, Lorelei was happy to hear that. "I can't even imagine where we're going from here," she said. "At least for the moment, it's peaceful. It's quiet, and I don't really feel like we're in any danger."

"And you could be wrong about that," Griffin said. "Not only do we have the normal problems but this particular area is well-known for pirates too."

She stiffened and stared at him in shock. "What?"

He nodded. "The good news is, armed security is on board just for that event."

"But that's ridiculous," Lorelei said, glancing around nervously. "It's like we're at the end of the ocean."

"It is what it is," he said with a nonchalance that surprised her.

"Surely we aren't getting blasé about pirates now, are we?"

"I'm more concerned about the men who kidnapped you two. Let's make sure that we get you home safe and sound with nobody even knowing that you made it there."

"You know we could have gone by private jet, right?"

"We could have," he said cheerfully. "But, as long as you're undercover and out of the way, you have no idea where we are and what we're doing. And neither do the kidnappers."

And just when she thought it was time for a nap, by the position of the afternoon sun, Griffin stood, gathered all the dishes, put it on the tray, motioned to Jax, and said, "It's time."

In a small voice, Lorelei asked, "Time for what?" She hated to admit it, but she was damn afraid that he would pull out scuba gear or something equally dangerous. She'd never been much of a water person, and this was getting scarier and a whole lot more dangerous than she'd first thought it would be.

He looked at her with a grin on his face and said, "You'll see."

And, beside her, something—small—came up out of the water. A round object, until the rest of it broke through. They were coming alongside a submarine. She bolted to her feet and stared in shock. "Oh, my God," she croaked.

"Just like Jax told you. *Underwater.*"

THE TRANSFER WAS made as quietly and as efficiently as possible. And the two girls were now safely in one bunk in a spare cabin on the supply deck. They had been led here by one seaman who made no conversation and neither did he expect any. Griffin noted the four bunks for the four of them. He settled into his lower bunk, placed his laptop underneath his bunk, with Jax already settled up above in the top bunk, and said, "We'll take a nap."

"A nap?" Amelia Rose asked. "Didn't you sleep last night?"

His lips quirked. "I did, indeed," he said, "but I have to be ready for whatever comes. So right now, it's an opportunity to grab some shut-eye." And he closed his eyes but couldn't sleep. It was also time for him to let his mind wander and to get all the information he had in his head organized and reorganized.

Besides the initial checks into Gerard, his previous wives, Lorelei, Nurse, and even Amelia Rose, they had further backgrounds on both sons, on the current wife, and on the brother and his family, but absolutely nothing pointed a finger at any one person. They were still working on the family connections.

Griffin had a suspicion it was all connected to the brother, but he had no proof. Just a question about a man who worked at his brother's company knowing it would never be fully his. Also the brother could be involved with yet another family member, but that led to the big question of, why partner up? Or was it to have the connections to pull this off? One had an idea but couldn't do it alone. Hence the need for the second party.

If so, then they must share the ransom money. That often didn't go well. Unless one partner wanted something much different than the other.

They'd done a deep search on Gerard's business holdings but had found nothing criminal or underhanded. And nothing involving Thailand, other than two of Gerard's companies were buying satellite time and looking at overhauling their global communication systems.

No, this felt like it was much closer than a business-related retaliation, even though that played into this, what with the security guard for the big arms dealer in Thailand being the original kidnapper. Yet they had not found a link between the original kidnapper and someone in Gerard's family. And yet, this was all about family. Griffin knew it in his gut. He had seen takeovers within a family happen before. A lot of times, the younger generation didn't want to wait for the older generation to retire. It usually had fatal consequences for the elder generation.

Gerard though, in this case, was hardly senile or even elderly. But, if his sons were looking for more power, more money, and more status, this would definitely be one way to get it. Both sons were married and, according to the details, have been for several years. No children yet in either marriage. And then there was Gerard's wife.

Griffin felt they were missing something. They were missing *somebody*.

On that note, he rolled over and looked at Lorelei. "Can you make me a list of everybody in the household?"

"Don't you have that already?" she asked without looking at him.

"I have an official one," he said, "but I want an unofficial one from an insider."

She looked over, puzzled.

He nodded. "So include boyfriends, girlfriends, delivery people, and anybody who you see on a regular basis at the house."

Understanding lit her chocolate-colored gaze. She nodded, reached into her bag on the floor for the personal notebook that she always kept with her, and started writing. As he watched, she had already written down more names than he expected. "Also write down in what capacity you know them as," he said. He dropped back onto his pillow, linked his fingers, and placed them under his head, while he continued to think about all the information swirling around in his thoughts.

He knew that Gerard didn't want to think it was anybody in the family, but Griffin was pretty sure Gerard was wrong. He rolled over, looked at Lorelei again, and said, "Add anything you know about his brother's family."

"He's married, has two sons of his own, and was there with Gerard right from the beginning. I'm sure you have intel on all these people," she said in exasperation, "so what difference does it make what I write down?"

He smiled. "Because you see things. You see things differently." And he rolled back over again.

He could hear her snort, but then Amelia Rose said, "He's right, you know? You do see things differently. Any time I get upset or get into an argument with Mom, you always point out another perspective to help me adjust."

"Well then, you help me with this list," Lorelei said. "Who do we see in the house all the time? Because you know that you and I are both invisible."

"That's true," Amelia Rose said. "But we also work on that."

Griffin sat up and looked at her. "What do you mean by that?"

She shrugged. "We work hard to not be seen a lot of the time."

"And why is that?"

"Because, if I go out, I get in trouble," she said with a conspiratorial grin to Lorelei. "My dad likes to think that I'm super smart because I spend hours and hours working on my books. But the thing is, I'm super smart because Lorelei teaches it to me, and I get it fast and easily. So then we have lots of free time, but I'm not allowed lots of free time." She rolled her eyes. "They want me to always work on something else. But I want to have fun too."

"And that all makes sense," he said. "So what do you do to appear invisible?"

She shrugged. "We're very good at listening for footsteps and hearing conversations using back staircases. Even a couple secret entrances and exits to the hallways are in the back."

"Interesting," he said. "I gather then the house that you live in is old."

"Built in the 1500s," she said with a big smile.

"Right. So then you should add people to the list too, Amelia Rose. Maybe you'll remember some who Lorelei forgot." He laid back down, thinking about what a life it was for the two of them. Part of the big machine, full of expectations, and then condemnation if the expectations weren't met. And what kind of a life was it for a child to go from study to study to study? She needed playtime and free time and time to think and time to just be. But then again, that was what life was often like in some of these wealthier families.

He half listened to the girls and half let his mind churn again. To him, it all boiled down to power. Somebody wanted something. Gerard wasn't willing to give it. They took his daughter instead. She was leverage, clear and simple. So, who wanted something from Gerard, and what was it that he wasn't willing to give?

He looked at the two girls. "What is one thing your father really wants in life?"

The two looked at him, nonplussed.

"Let me rephrase that," he said, capturing the angles in his head. "What is the one thing your father isn't willing to give up?"

"His company," Lorelei said instantly. "Power."

He looked over at Amelia Rose. "And do you agree with that?"

"Yes," she said. "But also me. Although, if I'm honest, I'm probably a close second."

He nodded. "Which is why you were kidnapped," he said. "Because you're a close second, so they're forcing him to make a choice. Give up his first choice and keep his second choice, or keep his first choice and lose his second choice. But, if he gives up power, he gets to keep you."

"But then the contest was already lost," Amelia Rose said sadly. "Remember that part about me being second choice?"

"That's how *you* feel," he said with emphasis. "But not necessarily how your father feels. He may not have the ability to show you that you're in first place, and he may not have had the time or the necessity to decide which was in first or second place until now."

"But surely, if it's something like power, once he's got his daughter back, he'll turn around and come after whoever did this," Lorelei said in confusion. "So, whoever is doing this has to make sure they have a loophole to get what they want and to stay safe themselves."

"Or not so much to stay safe," he said softly, "but to ensure ..." And then he left it hanging.

Lorelei looked at him for a long moment, puzzled, and then her eyes widened in knowledge. She moved closer to Griffin and whispered, "To make sure he can't come back after them. In other words, although we're in danger, so too is her father."

Amelia Rose watched them but didn't seem able to hear them.

Griffin nodded slowly. "And again I don't think it's a case of *we're in more danger than he is* or *he's in more danger than we are.* But it would look extremely suspicious if something happened after this kidnapping event that suddenly had Gerard out of the picture. If the masterminds behind all this were smart, they'd make it seem like an accident. Because really, if somebody can take both of them out of the equation, what happens to the company?"

"It goes to the sons, I would think," she whispered, curious. "But I don't know how the will is written."

"And let's not forget the brother is the vice president, so he would potentially move up or possibly get fired depending on how many shares he has ..."

She nodded slowly. "Can you send a warning to Gerard?"

At that, Jax swung down off his bunk and said, "I'm on it." And he walked out of the room.

As he left, Amelia Rose hopped to her feet and said,

"Can we leave the room? Can we go explore?"

"Unfortunately not," Griffin said. "That's not allowed." When she frowned at him, he shook his head. "By rights, Jax shouldn't have left either."

"We don't want him to get in trouble," Lorelei said.

Amelia Rose didn't bother with words. She raced to the door and tried to open it. When she found it locked, she turned to Griffin in shock. "Will they let him back in?"

Griffin nodded. "They will. He's not far. He'll be out in the hallway, talking to somebody."

"Oh," she said in a small voice.

He realized just how much stress was on her shoulders. He shouldn't have had this conversation when she was sitting here and listening, but, if she was as smart as everybody said, she needed to know that their danger was not something so easily avoided.

"Have you got that list for me?" he asked, looking over at Lorelei. "I've already sorted through information we have on the sons. They both started in the company as young men and worked their way up. Both are respected and well-liked. No hint of being upset that Dad hasn't stepped down yet. So not sure if they are hiding dissent really well or if there isn't any—or rather not much. All young men want to move up, and all men want to be Top Dog, but, while Gerard is there, there's no moving him down and out of the company. It would take something major for that to happen."

"What do you think? Is this everybody?" she asked Amelia Rose, who took a couple minutes to study the sheet and then nodded. Lorelei ripped it off the notepad and handed it to Griffin. He laid back down as Amelia Rose sat beside Lorelei.

"A lot of names are on here," he said. "Some I have never even heard of."

"That's because a lot of people are quiet in that house," Amelia Rose said defiantly. "They like to play games too."

"Games?"

She shrugged. "They're not allowed to be on the premises overnight in some cases, but Lorelei saw one of the maids who lives on the premises and has a boyfriend, and he comes and goes by the back entrance. The maid's boss doesn't like him, so he's not allowed to stay overnight, but he does anyway."

"I wonder if security knows about that?" Griffin muttered.

"That's only one of many instances," Lorelei said quietly. "A lot of the staff do leave and return at odd hours."

"Anything suspicious about it?" he asked.

She shrugged. "I don't think so, but again I don't know."

"Right," he said. It was interesting though. Griffin sat up and grabbed his laptop, checked to see if he had an internet signal, and then sent a text message asking for a moment of internet to send out intel. All communications and emissions were severely restricted on submarines so it might have to wait until they surfaced. He waited, and, sure enough, the chat window opened up, and he was given a black box to type in to. He quickly typed in all the names, one at a time, with the bits and pieces of information the girls had given him. As soon as he was done, the chat box closed, and the link severed.

He frowned, sat back, and said, "Well, we'll see if they can find any more information."

"If you have internet," Lorelei said, "can we use our laptops?"

He looked at her and said, "You can have your laptops but, once again, no outside access."

She stared at him. "Is that for our security or yours?"

He fixed a steady gaze on her. "Just by being here, we're putting hundreds of other men's and women's lives on the line. So my answer is that it is security for *everyone* aboard this sub."

CHAPTER 10

I F LORELEI HAD known how they were traveling, she would have been super excited about this opportunity. But it had happened so fast, and then she was escorted to stay in a room without any chance to even look around, and now she was stuck here. They were on their second day. And she had no clue how long it would be. The men were completely relaxed, taking the time as it passed easily, but, for her and Amelia Rose, time was not going quickly.

She looked at Griffin and asked, "How much longer?"

"Not long," he said.

She snorted. "Pretty sure you've told us that several times already."

"We'll be surfacing soonish."

She raised an eyebrow. "Hours, days, weeks, months, years?" she asked, ending on a caustic tone.

He grinned. "Hours."

Immediately Amelia Rose sat up and stared at him in shock. "Really?"

He nodded. "We're just waiting for the go-ahead."

Just then an odd sound ran through the submarine; Lorelei sat up and looked around. "What was that?" The angle of the people shifted.

He looked at her and said, "We're rising."

She stared at him, then looked around, feeling the sub

rise up to the surface. "Are you sure we couldn't have a tour, even a little one?"

He shook his head. "Not in any way, shape, or form."

Her shoulders sagged. "Are you blindfolding us to get us up and out?"

"No, but nobody else will see us." His phone buzzed. He looked down, nodded, and said, "Let's go."

"What if we weren't packed?" she asked in a curt tone.

"We didn't give you a choice," Jax said, stepping in. "We never know from one day to the next. Now we know, and it's a good thing that you followed our instructions and stay packed."

And, sure enough, they had everything. They were told to repack to be ready to go at a moment's notice, which is why the last couple days had seemed almost anticlimactic. But, with Jax in front, Griffin behind, and Amelia Rose between them, they were led out and back up to the surface. As Lorelei stood here, staring at the ocean around them with just the bare minimum of the sub showing, she was astonished. But right in front of them was a different ship. She looked at it and asked, "And how are we getting on that?"

Griffin tapped her shoulder, and she turned around. A small pontoon boat waited for them. They were quickly transferred to the small boat and then moved out to the larger one. As they made the transfer yet again, Amelia Rose laughed and said, "This has been fun. How long will we be on this ship?"

"Not long," he said. "We're taking a helicopter again."

It was like a replay, only in reverse of their trip out.

"At least you seem to know what you're doing," she said. She was grateful to be off the sub. And, more than that, she was just grateful to have been released from the prison of that small enclosed room. It hadn't been that bad, but they'd been tired and waiting on edge, knowing that they could be moving at any time. They were led up to the top of the current ship, which she had no clue what it even was. It looked like a small tanker, but a helicopter landing pad was on the top deck, with a helicopter waiting for them. She looked at Griffin. "Takes a lot to set up something like this."

He nodded. They rushed onto the helicopter, and it took off almost immediately. And as it went high in the sky, she could look out and see land in the distance. She shook her head. "I have no clue where we are."

"Not a problem," Griffin said. "You will soon."

She snorted. But, when the helicopter settled down on the landing pad of Gerard's home, she cried out in surprise. "I had no clue we were so close," she said. As soon as the rotors slowed enough, several men raced from the estate toward them. The helicopter doors were open, and all four of them were escorted off and quickly led into the house.

There, Amelia Rose turned, looking around. "We're home again," she cried out. As soon as she was inside, she ran through the front hallway, calling out, "Poppy! Poppy!"

Double doors opened, and a man strode toward them. As soon as his gaze fell on his daughter, Lorelei could see the love pouring from his face. He opened his arms, and Amelia Rose ran into them. He picked her up and hugged her close, then twirled her around, holding back the tears. She knew Gerard was an emotional man. Usually they only saw his negative emotions though—not this side.

Lorelei glanced at Griffin and Jax and whispered, "See? He really does care."

"Absolutely he does," Jax said.

"The question is, who's using that to get what they

want?" Griffin asked.

She didn't even want to hazard a guess. After a few minutes of hugging his daughter, Gerard walked over, still with Amelia Rose in his arms, her legs wrapped around his waist as she beamed at Griffin and Jax.

"This is my poppy," Amelia Rose said.

Gerard held out his hand and shook both of the men's hands vigorously. "Thank you so much," he said.

Jax nodded but didn't say anything.

Griffin shook his hand and said, "You're welcome."

Gerard's gaze dropped to Lorelei. He smiled and wrapped an arm around her shoulders and hugged her up close. "I can't believe what you two have been through," he said.

Lorelei stepped back, smiled up at him, and said, "Don't mind if the next time you want to send me to Thailand, I refuse."

He rolled his eyes at that, his face hardening. "Nobody's going anywhere until we know what's going on."

"Good," Griffin said, "because we need to talk."

Gerard looked at him solemnly, then focused on the girls and said, "Let's get you guys to your rooms."

Lorelei desperately wanted to stay with the men so she could hear the details but had the feeling they would be put into their place as to where *the women belong*.

But Griffin surprised her. "I think Lorelei needs to hear this too."

Gerard frowned at him. "What does she have to do with any of this?"

"Outside of being a victim and potentially could still be a victim," Griffin said, his tone brooking no argument, "she needs to know how much danger you're all still in."

"Not her surely," Gerard asked, his arms crossing as he geared up for his more belligerent and domineering wouldn't-budge manner.

Lorelei shook her head. "It's okay, Griffin," she said. "You can fill me in later."

He frowned, not liking her answer, but nodded.

As she turned to walk away, she stopped and said, "Please don't leave without speaking with me," and waited until both men nodded. And then she grabbed Amelia Rose's hand and said, "Let's go unpack our bags."

"But I want to stay with them," Amelia Rose said.

"Amelia Rose, don't you argue," her father ordered.

She turned and glared at him. "You're not the one who was tossed into vehicles and locked up in hotels and treated like you were nothing," she shouted at him. "We have a right to know what's happening now."

Surprised and maybe even astonished at the suddenly disruptive manner of his daughter, Gerard frowned at her. But Lorelei stepped in and said, "She is overwrought. We have been kept abreast of everything up until now. It would help her mind to calm down if she understood that we were safe now."

"Of course we're safe," Gerard said, bewildered. "She's home."

"But you don't know a lot of things yet, like whether or not the reason that we were kidnapped started here," Amelia Rose said, and then she turned and ran away.

Offering an apologetic smile, Lorelei followed her charge. She knew that the men would have a heck of a conversation coming up. She had a good idea what Griffin wanted to say, but way too many uncertain elements were involved. Gerard needed a man-to-man talk. She almost laughed at that. Because if ever there was a position that kept the women in *the women's place*, it was this one.

It's not that she would ever succumb to that mentality, and it bothered her that Amelia Rose was being raised with that mentality, so Lorelei had done what she could to let Amelia Rose know that her opinion matters and what she had to say mattered. Nothing was quite so easy as letting the world dominate you so that you became a silent victim by just not even speaking up.

It wouldn't be an easy conversation in the office. Gerard was very particular about dealing with matters concerning his family. He was also a bit of a control freak, and no way would he entertain any implication that somebody else close to him was involved in this nightmare.

She wished she could be a fly on the wall.

"WHAT IS IT you want to speak to me about?" Gerard asked in a more genial tone than he had expressed at the onset. He motioned at the two visitor chairs in his office and took his spot behind his imposing oak desk. It was a power play to make them feel uncomfortable, but Griffin hadn't lived in this world for as long as he had to allow something like that to throw him.

"We think the kidnapping is connected to your family," he said bluntly.

Gerard's gaze widened, and he shook his head. "No way in hell."

"What happens if you die?"

His eyebrows rose. "The estate's fairly convoluted," he said. "There's no simple answer. It's not as if my wife gains everything up on my death."

"Of course not. What about the company? How does that get divided up?"

Gerard's fingers pounded on the desk as he thrummed them. "My sons get an equal share. My brother stays on as the vice president, and he has a small voting block. He doesn't gain much more."

"Interesting," Griffin said. "So what happens if you willingly sign over more shares to a third party or a fourth party?"

"*Willingly* would mean that I'm handing off some of my control. Not happening."

"How much do your sons each have now?"

"Twenty percent," he said, "and I have fifty. Actually fifty-one and then my brother has nine."

"So your fifty-one gets split evenly?"

"No, not quite," he said, "twenty-five goes to my daughter, the remainder is split by my sons with my brother getting a little more—six, I think."

"Oh, now that's interesting. So your brother goes from nine to fifteen, and then each of the sons end up with thirty."

"Something like that, yes. Why is that interesting? They have to work together to make the company still work."

"And, for that reason, I'm wondering if somebody in there hasn't thrown in his shares with somebody else."

Gerard stared at him in shock. "The only way any of that'll happen is if I'm not here to keep control, so the question is moot."

"Well, not if somebody decides to take you *and* your daughter out, either together, separately, as an accident or a brazen attempt at ownership of the company."

Gerard sank back into his big chair and studied him. "I face death almost weekly," he said. "There was no reason to take my daughter this time instead."

"For the ransom. Except, now that they didn't succeed, their plan A is a wash. Did you, by the way, take the money to the drop as planned?"

He shrugged and nodded. "But nobody picked it up."

"I'm not surprised," he said. "Did you actually take the twenty-five million?"

He shook his head. "I took some, like one hundred thousand, but the rest was fake."

"And so the kidnapper could have known it was fake and didn't show up for that reason?"

"I don't like what you're thinking," he said, "but you can bet only a select few knew anything about this. I don't know how many agents of the MI6 department would have known, but I highly doubt too many people did."

"Did your sons know?"

He nodded.

"Your brother?"

He nodded.

"Your wife?"

"Of course my wife, for God's sake. It's her daughter."

"So, all of the same intimate family members knew that you were lying to and cheating the kidnapper even at this point."

"I don't lie and cheat at any point," he said. "We knew it was a bluff, but I didn't want to take the chance."

"So there was no sign of anybody at any point in time coming to pick up the money?"

"Not that we could tell, no. MI6 ran the cameras all around the area. Nobody came before, and nobody came twenty-four hours afterward."

"Good to know," Griffin said. He turned to look at Jax. "That proves our theory, doesn't it?"

Jax nodded slowly. "It does. It's clearly an inside job."

CHAPTER 11

T HE GIRLS COULD hear Gerard's roar from the bottom of the stairwell where they were still lugging their luggage up to the first landing—something Lorelei encouraged so that Amelia Rose learned to be self-sufficient, not relying on staff to help her at all times. Lorelei stopped, looked at Amelia Rose, and whispered, "Oh, that didn't go well."

Amelia Rose shook her head. "He doesn't like whatever they're telling him."

"Isn't that the truth," she said. She quickly grabbed Amelia Rose's bags. "Come on. Let's go upstairs. We don't want to be caught out here if they leave the office."

Amelia Rose raced ahead of Lorelei while she struggled with all the luggage. Now she knew how Jax and Griffin felt. She'd let them carry everything, but now it was up to her. Finally upstairs, she took the two pieces of luggage that were her bags to her room and then carried Amelia Rose's luggage to hers. They quickly unpacked, tossing into the laundry cart what needed to be washed and putting away their luggage.

"Let's go put on laundry too." It was something that Lorelei often did, which was especially convenient with a laundry room on the same floor, even though the housekeepers came in and changed the bedding. Amelia Rose's mother used to come in and criticize the quality of their clothing and whether it was time for them to be tossed rather than be washed. But, not giving anybody a chance to tell her otherwise, Lorelei quickly put Amelia Rose's clothes into the washer and started it. She'd like to do the same for hers but that would have to be the mixed load.

She still heard loud voices downstairs. She wondered if she should find out what the heck was going on. Amelia Rose looked nervous, chewing on her bottom lip, as she stared down the hall toward the stairway.

"I wonder where your mother is?" Lorelei asked suddenly. "I'm sure she's waiting to hear news of your arrival."

Amelia Rose turned, looked up at her. "I'll call her." Lorelei held out her phone, and Amelia Rose called her mother. But it simply rang and rang and rang.

Seeing the despondent sag to the little girl's shoulders, Lorelei reached out and hugged her. "You know what? She's probably out riding."

At that, Amelia Rose nodded. "That's where she'll be. Or maybe in the barn." She brightened. "We should go to the barn and surprise her."

Knowing how that was definitely not a good idea—Wendy was carrying on an affair with one of the trainers—Lorelei shook her head and said, "You wouldn't like to surprise her if she's napping, would you?"

"She wouldn't be napping in the barn," Amelia Rose said. "I'm not a child anymore. Unfortunately I've seen way too much of the world already. What you're saying is, she's probably having sex with one of the stable hands, aren't you?" There was such disdain in her voice that Lorelei had to laugh. It was also typical of Amelia Rose to be so blunt when she wanted to be.

"Well, she certainly might be," she said. "Either way, we

won't disturb her."

Amelia Rose nodded and then said, "But I still want to know what they're yelling about downstairs."

"I do too," Lorelei said. "It has to do with our kidnapping."

"Then we have every right to find out," Amelia Rose protested. And, precocious as always, she raced ahead of Lorelei and slipped into one of the hallways that led to a second staircase. It would take them around behind Gerard's office. Lorelei, not wanting her charge to go off on her own, followed her. She tried calling her, but her voice carried too loudly. Instead, she picked up her feet and ran behind her.

When she finally caught up to her charge, she crept down the stairs on the far side of the office, looking for the bolt-holes they both knew were here. As soon as Amelia Rose found one, she gasped, her face plastered against the wall, spying through the small hole. Immediately Lorelei stepped up to one of the higher ones and looked in. Amelia Rose's father still ranted and raved, stomping about the office like a madman, yelling at the two men both sitting relaxed in the chairs, half looking at each other and half ignoring the tirade enacted out all around them.

Finally Gerard came to a stop, wiped his mouth, then ran his fingers through his hair. "You're wrong," he stated firmly. "I know you are wrong." His voice kept rising on every word. "I refuse to listen to any more of this wild talk against my family," he roared.

Lorelei wasn't sure Jax and Griffin were ever wrong in their world. She was pretty darn sure that they knew exactly what they were doing at all times. It was a little disconcerting actually. Not to mention the fact that they seemed to know so much about everyone. Of course, she hadn't helped when she had deliberately given out more names of staff and visitors in the household too.

But, if it came to keeping Amelia Rose safe, Lorelei would do anything she could. Not that the people on her list would appreciate it. It seemed like nobody ever did. Still, that wasn't her problem. She was bound and determined to keep Amelia Rose as safe as she could. She watched Gerard walk around, sit down at his desk, and bury his face in his hands.

He finally lifted his face and said, "You're wrong. You need to go over your so-called evidence again."

Griffin shook his head, launched to his feet, and said, "No, we're not wrong, but you don't want anything to do with our intel? That's fine. But it's up to you then to keep your daughter and her tutor safe. And to watch your own back."

"Of course I'll keep them safe," he said in exasperation.

"And how do you expect to do that?" Jax asked, standing at a slower rate. "When it's quite likely the threats are coming from within your own family."

"Says you," Gerard said, glaring at both of them. "I thank you for bringing my daughter and Lorelei back home again. But I want you to leave now."

Griffin nodded. "No problem." And he turned and marched from the office.

Amelia Rose gasped and said, "We have to stop them."

Lorelei admitted she didn't want them to leave either, but it was beyond her control. She did, however, want to say goodbye to them.

Amelia Rose raced away and slipped through one of the bookshelves on the library side and ran toward the front door. As she got there, the men walked through the front entrance. One of the manservants closed it behind them. Amelia Rose raced to the front door, but the manservant stepped in front. She screamed, "Get out of the way. I have to say goodbye."

He lifted his head and looked down the hallway, watching Lorelei coming up behind her. Lorelei saw Gerard also coming down the hallway, giving a clipped nod. The manservant stepped aside and opened the front door.

Amelia Rose launched herself outside, Lorelei following her very quickly. Jax picked up Amelia Rose and hugged her carefully. Then Amelia Rose threw herself at Griffin. She shook her head and said, "Poppy shouldn't be so mean to you."

Both men chuckled, and Jax said, "Don't you worry about it, pumpkin. We're fine."

"But we might not be," Amelia Rose cried out. "I don't trust anyone here."

Griffin crouched in front of her. Even though she was eleven, he understood full well that she needed some reassurance. He grabbed both her hands and said, "You can always call us if you run into trouble."

"And how will we do that? You didn't give us your numbers."

Lorelei joined them, coming up behind her charge. She reached out a hand and shook Jax's and said formally, "Thank you so much." And then she reached out to Griffin, but he glared at her and said, "Don't you dare." And the look in his eyes glinted with determination. She let her hand drop, gave him a smile, and said, "It's awkward now."

"Not awkward at all," he said, and he snagged her chin, tilted it up, and kissed her hard. Shaken more by the emotions rolling inside her and the sense of loss already forming, she just stared at him when he pulled away.

"We don't have your numbers," Amelia Rose called out again.

Griffin reached inside his wallet, pulled out a piece of paper, and handed it to Lorelei. "Put that number into your phone, and have Amelia Rose memorize my number as well," he said. "Call that number and ask for me anytime you need to. Or rather, just say you're in trouble, and I'll come."

"But what if they move us somewhere else?" Amelia Rose asked, determined to not be reassured that he wouldn't break contact.

"I'll find you," he said, gently stroking her arm where her chip was. The arm band had already been removed. "Just like I did last time." Then he raised his gaze to look at Lorelei and whispered, "I promise."

She clutched the paper in her hand and turned to look up at Jax. She wanted to say something but didn't know what, and her shoulders fell helplessly as she struggled to control her emotions while her tears threatened. He gently stroked her cheek. "Look after her."

She nodded. "Look after yourselves." And she watched, already groaning, as they both walked away.

Amelia Rose had no intention of staying calm or quiet about it. She turned and raced back inside, yelling at her father, "You can't let them leave."

"Hush now, Amelia Rose," he said, his voice stern, but his arms going around her in a hug. "You don't know what's going on."

She pulled out of his arms and glared up at him. "I know more than you think. Yes, I'm still a child, but I'm not that much of a child any longer," she said bitterly. "They rescued us, and they kept us safe all this time. They know what's going on."

"But you don't," he reiterated. "Now, isn't it time for you to have a nap?"

Lorelei sighed quietly. It was such a typical thing for Gerard to say. He had absolutely no idea how to deal with his daughter.

"I doubt I'll ever sleep again, particularly in this house," Amelia Rose yelled as she stormed up the stairs. However, she stopped at the first landing and yelled again. "Poppy, it's you who doesn't understand. I think people might be mad about me getting thirty-five percent of the company."

Lorelei gasped and stopped abruptly. *Oh, my God. This changes everything.* Once again Lorelei followed her charge, as was her job. *I need to tell Griffin …* Yet she would be abruptly ending her assignment as Amelia Rose's tutor if she did that. She couldn't abandon Amelia Rose now. Her emotions were all stirred up from being kidnapped. And she hadn't even reached puberty yet, when an avalanche of emotions would truly hit her. Lorelei couldn't imagine how things would be when Amelia Rose hit that age. She was already a bundle of nerves now and would need lots of support to get her through this event.

Even if I tell Gerard first, … he will send me away, just like he did Griffin and Jax.

As Lorelei reached the first landing, Gerard called to her, "Lorelei, I'd like a few moments in the office with you, please."

She hesitated. She had to do what she must to save Amelia Rose. Even if it meant giving up her own relationship with the precious girl. Lorelei swallowed her tears, turned, and then nodded. "Right now?"

He nodded, but it was a crisp and clean nod. A determined nod.

And her heart sank. But her spine became steel as she stood up taller. She slowly walked back down the stairs, feeling a sudden sense of doom as she followed him into his office. Instinctively she took Griffin's spot in his chair and asked, "What can I help you with?"

"Was my daughter touched in any way?" he asked bleakly.

She shook her head. "No, she wasn't." She could see the relief wash over his features.

He nodded again. "I'm really glad to hear that. Is there any chance she might have been, and you didn't know?"

She shook her head. "I've been with her all the time. We were never separated. She was always in my sight. However, she has changed and is very emotional after having Nurse killed in front of her. That event alone will be a trauma she'll struggle with," she said bluntly. "You cannot mitigate all the damage done to her psyche from that event alone."

"Poor Mary. She was the most loving woman." Gerard sank back into his chair. "I wish Amelia Rose hadn't seen that. Who would traumatize a child like that?"

"I wish she had never seen that too," she said. "Hell, I wish I hadn't seen it."

"Nurse suffered at the end, didn't she?"

"Yes," Lorelei said, wincing and shoving her own memories back down again, "she did. There's no easy way to say it. She was terrified. She'd been held until we were returned to the room, and, at that point in time, she was used as a lesson to make us comply with their wishes." She didn't explain how Nurse had urged them to leave, going separate ways, when the chance had presented itself. Even though Lorelei had argued, Nurse had been adamant. She wouldn't be able to keep up, and the two girls could return and rescue her. Instead, none of the women had gotten away, and Nurse had paid the ultimate price.

"Did they beat her up?"

She didn't know why he wanted to torment himself with the details, but a lot of people needed to know everything before they had enough closure to walk away. "They certainly hit her a couple times, but I don't think they did much more than tie her up and maybe threaten her beforehand. However, when we walked in, they proceeded to hit her several times," she said bleakly. "I tried to stop them, and they hit me too. And then I tried to stop Amelia Rose from going to Nurse. That I did manage, but not before they threatened to hurt your daughter as well. And then they said, as a punishment for us escaping, and to make sure we didn't do it again, they had to kill Nurse."

Gerard sat there, his jaw working for a long moment; then he said, "Thank you."

"I wish I could have saved her," she said. "They knew exactly who she was and her relationship to Amelia Rose. She was targeted. We all were but Nurse particularly."

At that, he looked at her in surprise. "Do you really think so?"

She nodded. "I do."

"Do you think this whole thing was about Nurse and not about Amelia Rose?"

"I hadn't considered it from that viewpoint." She tilted her head to one side. "I think that the end result was always supposed to be that Nurse died," she said, slowly formulating her thoughts. "I think that Amelia Rose was also supposed to remain as a captive. For blackmail first, then as leverage for you to do something that the kidnappers wanted."

"And yet, the ransom note was for just money."

"But they didn't pick it up, did they?"

He sat back and studied her. "Did you talk to the two men about this?"

"There wasn't anything else to talk about," she said wearily. "They asked question upon question. And yet, almost everything they said made sense to me too."

"You surely can't think that Amelia Rose's brothers or uncle or mother are involved in this, do you?"

"Nurse's death was personal," she said. "I can't imagine that anybody would have just killed her to teach us a lesson. Obviously I don't understand people like this at all, so maybe that's normal behavior among evil men, but they did not at any time hurt Amelia Rose."

"Was this marriage stuff just all bullshit then?" he asked, worried.

She could see that still the sexual abuse aspect bothered him.

"Likely," she said, "just more emotional torture to overpower you. To traumatize you more."

"Maybe," he said, "but nobody's tried to shift anything within the company. The stocks are down slightly but not crashing. There hasn't been an aggressive buyout or any takeover maneuver. Nothing on a business level."

"I don't think it's business-related in the sense of a takeover by another business or corporation," she said, tiptoeing around the issue. "I think it's all personal."

"But what can anybody possibly gain from this?" he asked, crying out. "I already suffered through this with my son. I shouldn't have to suffer through it with my daughter."

"Which is why she made the perfect weapon," Lorelei said gently. "You're already primed to do anything to keep your daughter safe and to not relive what happened all those years ago."

He stared at her and then pinched the bridge of his nose. "You're right," he said. "You're very right. The trouble is, a lot of people would know what had happened to me already. So it wouldn't take much digging to figure out how to get to me."

"But would they understand how much it devastated you?" *Like Nurse would know. ... And like Wendy would know ...*

He shook his head, waved one hand, but never responded to that question. "Even if I was asked to step down from the companies," he said, "once I got my daughter back, obviously I'd turn around and retaliate."

"Unless they permanently stopped you from retaliating."

He raised his head and looked at her, and she nodded. "And that's why you shouldn't have sent Griffin and Jax away. They firmly believe that your life is in as much danger as Amelia Rose's."

He stared at her, and his face turned gray. "I don't even care about my life, but I do care about hers."

"Imagine if both of you were dead," she said. "A house fire, a car accident, a drowning ..."

"You mean, together?"

She nodded. "You already told the men how the company divides down and that your sons' holdings and your brother's increases, but what about Amelia Rose? If she's living, does she get a portion of the business?"

"She gets a share, as do her brothers," he said softly. "My brother's share is not that much."

"But that was the previous distribution upon your death. ... Did you change your will recently?" she asked.

"Did you make any announcement recently? Did you ever have a new conversation about how the estate would break down upon your death?"

"Yes," he said bleakly. "We had a family meeting about it."

She stayed quiet and waited. "And now, looking back on that family meeting, did you think that maybe some people didn't like what you had to say?"

"Possibly," he said. "But I don't want to believe it's any of them."

"And what if just you died? Each one of them, instead of gaining in power actually loses power, don't they?"

He shook his head. "How is that possible?"

"Because that fifty-one percent that you call *yours* must really be twenty-five percent Amelia Rose's and twenty-six percent yours, right?"

"How do you know that?"

"It's the only way she can end up with thirty-five percent of the business at your death."

Gerard was speechless, which was a rare event.

"She listens to everything you say while she spends the day in your office with you. She's quite a remarkable child and has a great business sense for an eleven-year-old. But you already know that, don't you? You've been grooming her, haven't you? Otherwise you wouldn't have given her a controlling interest in the company upon your death."

Gerard ran his fingers through his hair.

"While you're alive, she can't take part in the company, correct?"

"Of course not. She's a child."

At this point, Lorelei leaned forward and asked, "So, while you are alive, you vote her portion until she becomes of age. And, at your death, she gains ten percent, giving her thirty-five percent—*the* controlling interest in the company. Your sons bump up to twenty-five percent each, your brother to fifteen percent. So, if you should die, who would vote Amelia Rose's controlling portion?"

His jaw dropped as he stared at her, and he said, "Her mother." Then he shook his head. "Hell, no. There's no way she would do anything to hurt Amelia Rose."

"I have nothing to say about that, except to remind you that no one hurt Amelia Rose *physically*," Lorelei said. "And I think you're taking an ugly chance sending those two men away. You don't know who all is involved. Since you ruined the kidnappers' chance at twenty-five million, they may feel pressured to create your accidental death, so they have access to not only *all* your money but also *all* your businesses."

He groaned, grabbed his phone, and called somebody. "Bring them back," he said harshly. Then he tossed his phone down and said, "Those men could be part of the problem."

"They could be," she said drily. "But I highly doubt they want to torture themselves looking after a terrorized young woman and an emotionally fragile child any longer than they have to."

"I gather you weren't the most cooperative."

"We were once we realized they were on our side," she said, "but you have to understand how we both have a lot of trauma that we're facing from the two different kidnappings. Crying, emotional females, having nightmares, not sleeping well, are difficult for these men to handle too."

He nodded. "I'm sorry. I never even thought to ask, but did they hurt you physically?"

"I was hit across the face a couple times," she said, "but

the nightmares ..." She stood, smiled at him, and said, "If you don't mind, I need to keep an eye on Amelia Rose. She's very emotional right now."

"Well, tell her that I've got the men coming back," he said. "Maybe that will make her feel better."

"You mean, you've asked somebody to *request* that the men return," she said. "They don't take orders very well from other people. And I'm sure they make decisions on their own—not because you say so."

"Men like that never take orders."

"I agree with you there," she said. And, with a smile, she turned and walked out, but her heart was lighter to realize that maybe, just maybe, she'd keep her job. *And* she might see Griffin again. She would sleep much better knowing that they were here, and she knew Amelia Rose would too. Lorelei didn't know if the wife had planned this kidnapping event or if Gerard's brother or sons were involved in this mess. But now she was suspicious of them all.

Either way, it didn't matter what Lorelei felt because it was all a massive betrayal for Gerard. He'd spent his life building this business and doing his best for his family. It had to suck to think that the betrayal was from within. But that's how life was sometimes. If it was worth doing, it was usually worth doing in a big way. And these people had obviously gone all in. The worst-case scenario would be if it were more than one of them.

As soon as she found Amelia Rose in her bed, Lorelei wrapped her arms around the girl and said, "Your dad asked Jax and Griffin to come back."

Immediately Amelia Rose hopped to her feet, turned, and looked at her. "Really?"

Lorelei nodded. "Yes. I haven't heard if they've agreed to

return or not though. But if we're lucky, they will."

"Call them," Amelia Rose demanded. "Tell them just in case they don't want to listen to Poppy. They'll come if you ask them."

Lorelei laughed. "No, they probably won't."

"Try, please," Amelia Rose said.

Hating to say no, Lorelei pulled out her phone and the piece of paper with Griffin's number on it and quickly dialed. When she heard Griffin's voice on the other side, she said, "Gerard asked some of his men to bring you back."

Griffin snorted. "That's nice. We're already miles down the road."

"Come back," Amelia Rose yelled into the phone. "Please, please, come back."

"Why?" Griffin asked. "Is there a problem?"

"Probably," Lorelei said. "I just spent the time since you left in the office with Gerard, helping him to see that maybe this is personal. If it isn't us in danger, I think he is."

"Then he has his own security staff," Griffin said in exasperation. But she could hear the two men talking. "We're on our way back," he said, "but if we get kicked out again …"

"I'll take the blame," she said. "I was there when he called his men and said to go get you."

She could hear the laughter in his voice when he said, "May not make a difference."

"No, but you're made of sterner stuff. I doubt he'll scare you away."

"Maybe not," he said. "And maybe I'm just coming so I can see you again."

"Well then, you should come when I have days off," she said.

"Do you get those?" he asked.

"Well, I used to. I have no idea what I'm supposed to do now."

"You can't leave me," Amelia Rose called out nervously. She knew that Griffin could hear the child's voice too; she was certainly loud enough.

"As you can tell," Lorelei said drily, "things are still in an upheaval here." She grabbed Amelia Rose's hand and walked over to the far side of the room where they could sit on the window bench. She motioned outside and said, "It's beautiful outside. After we're done talking to Griffin, we'll go for a walk, okay?"

"Over to the barn? To see if Mom's done her thing with the stable hand?"

Catching Griffin's snort on the phone, Lorelei winced and said, "We don't talk about her like that. Remember?"

"Fine," she said, "but that's only if Griffin comes back. And he has to bring Jax with him too."

"He doesn't *have* to do anything," Lorelei scolded. "Where are your manners?"

But Amelia Rose just sat in the corner and said, "Please get them to come home."

Into the phone, Lorelei said, "Did you hear that?"

"Yes," he said, "but you know we can't stay on as babysitters, right?"

"I know," she said, "but it would be nice if you had a day or two off that would line up with mine."

"That is an entirely different story." His voice deepened as he spoke, then became more businesslike as he added, "When we near the master gate again is where we find out if we're allowed back in or not."

"If it doesn't open, I'm sorry. It would mean that he had

called one of his men as a ploy to keep me appeased."

"And I'm sure a lot of men in this world would do a lot to make you happy."

"No, that's not the relationship I have with Gerard. But he would take my advice, especially if I said it was necessary for his daughter's peace of mind."

"And it is," Amelia Rose snapped from beside her. "If they won't let them into the gate, I'll override it and let them in myself." And, with that, Amelia Rose darted off.

"And I'm on the run behind her again." She ran behind her charge all the way down the staircase. "She has more energy than a filly, and I'm feeling very much like an old gray mare," she said sadly. "But, Griffin, she *just* told me that, under Gerard's new will, she would get thirty-five percent, *the* controlling interest."

"That changes everything."

"I know."

The wait was excruciating but finally through the windows of the front door, she would be able to see the gate opening, letting Griffin back in. "What vehicle are you driving?"

"One of our own," he said. "Why?"

"So your team already knew that you were here?"

"Of course," he said. "Why wouldn't they?"

"I don't know," she said. "It just seemed odd that you would already have new wheels."

He laughed. "We get what we need at any time. Remember?"

She smiled and said, "I remember." Then, on impulse, she said, "Too bad you don't need me."

And she hung up.

GRIFFIN FILLED IN Jax with the piece of the puzzle that Amelia Rose had supplied and studied his partner. "What do you think?" Just then his phone buzzed. He looked down, groaned, and said, "It's Gerard." He answered the call with a "Yes" in a noncommittal tone of voice.

"I need you boys to come back here."

Silence. Griffin glanced at Jax, who raised his eyebrows, stared back at him, and shrugged.

"I'm pretty sure our job's done," Griffin said.

"Maybe," Gerard said. "But it appears that Lorelei thinks you're a very necessary part of solving this, keeping the girls safe."

"Maybe, but she's not the boss in this situation, is she?" He couldn't help the cool tone in his voice. It's not as if Gerard had been terribly friendly at the end.

"No," Gerard said a heavy sigh. "But she seems to believe as you do."

That shot his eyebrows up. "Interesting," he said. "I can't say we've discussed it very much."

"No, but she's very intelligent. That's one of the reasons I hired her to tutor Amelia Rose. I do respect her brainpower."

Griffin found that interesting too. "And what is it you're asking us to do?"

"I'm asking you to come back and to help me get to the bottom of this."

"I'll have to talk to my boss about that," Griffin said.

"Don't bother," Gerard said. "It's already cleared. All you have to do is turn your vehicle around and get your asses back here." And, with that, he hung up.

Griffin looked at Jax and said, "Well, apparently Lorelei does have some influence."

"Probably Lorelei and more so Amelia Rose."

He nodded. "I guess we're going back."

"Odd how Gerard knew who to call up the ranks of the Mavericks, and yet, I don't think we have a *boss* to even ask, do we?"

Griffin shrugged. "Just a stalling tactic on my part," he said. "I didn't want him to think that we were jumping at the idea."

"Except that we *are* jumping at the idea," Jax said.

"Well, I am. You don't have to," he said.

"No, no. I'm in this to the end, whatever end that may be."

"Meaning, the little girl got to you?"

Instantly Jax turned it around and said, "Meaning, Lorelei got to you?"

"Well, that's true," he said. "She certainly did."

Jax laughed. "At least you admit it. That's a whole lot easier than ignoring it."

"She's not somebody you can ignore," he said.

"No, she isn't. Particularly when you're on hyperalert when she's around."

"And, like you said, it's not necessarily a good thing."

"No, but, with Gerard's *request*, and Amelia Rose's big announcement, I think it's well past the point of having a choice now, isn't it?"

"It so is." Griffin groaned and said, "Still feels like, you know, somebody calling an untamed puppy to come."

"That's just Gerard. We don't *have* to go," Jax said, "but it would be nice to get that chance to tell him, *I told you so.*"

Griffin laughed. "There is that."

"Plus you and I both know those girls are in danger. *And* the jerk Gerard."

"Oh, no," Griffin said. "There's no way we're *not* going. And I'm glad that he was forced to call us back. Let's hope we're not too late even now."

"And that's the thing, isn't it?" Jax said. "We don't even know where *all* the threats are coming from, but we do know that there *are* threats. Multiple threats to deal with."

"Yes," he said, "that sucks. However, we do know where *one* of those threats is coming from now."

It took them another twenty minutes to return to the mansion. And as soon as they arrived, Amelia Rose raced toward them and threw herself into their arms. Jax chuckled, picked her up, and said, "You know we can't keep doing this, right?"

She nodded. "Just until we keep Poppy safe."

Jax squeezed her tight and passed her off to Griffin.

Griffin loved the fact that she was half woman, yet half child. Still wanted to be hugged and picked up and tossed around, and yet, also wanted to be treated like an adult. She was a mature eleven-year-old in many ways, and yet, just a young child in so many others. No sooner had Griffin put Amelia Rose down than Gerard stepped out the front door too.

He walked to meet them, shook the men's hands, and said, "I apologize." His voice was stiff, but at least he was doing what he should do. "And, yes, please, let's go in and have another talk."

"No problem," Griffin said. "Maybe Lorelei should take part in it this time."

Gerard winced. "I've already heard her point of view. Everybody appears to think that it's a family matter and that

I'm in danger as well."

"Where is your wife?" Griffin asked.

"She's taken a short holiday to Venice."

Griffin and Jax exchanged a knowing glance.

"And I presume you've buffed up your security?" Jax said.

"I have," he said. "But, if what you say is true, how do I know who is loyal to me?"

"While we're in place," Griffin said, "we'll sort that out so you have a trustworthy team going forward."

"That's a good idea," he said with relief. "Let's start with my head of security. If he's clear, we can assign a lot of the other clearances to him."

"Good idea."

Back in the office, he ordered coffee for everyone, and they sat down, taking a good look at who they had on his security staff. Sixteen men were assigned across all the family members.

"Any idea if anybody's in financial distress or has a weakness that can be exploited?" Jax asked immediately.

"I wouldn't have thought so," Gerard said, "and that is my head of security's job."

"Which is why we'll check him out first," Griffin said. "He's in a position to put people in place as he wants and not necessarily people who are good for you."

"And that's a disturbing thought," Gerard said. "In my business, I hire the best that I can for the rest of this stuff. Nobody can look after everything."

"No," Jax said. "And the more widespread and diverse you become, the more you have to rely on others. As soon as you do, that's when you can end up in trouble."

Gerard nodded. He brought out files from the nearby

filing cabinet and said, "These are personnel files on everybody I currently employ in my security force, and the head of security's folder is on the top."

Jax looked at the name, chuckled, and said, "I know this guy."

"Do you?" Gerard looked at him and raised an eyebrow. "By reputation?"

"Yes," Jax said. "Up until this moment in time, I've never had any question about him." Jax reviewed the file quickly and then handed it to Griffin.

Griffin looked at it briefly, nodded, and said, "Except for one thing."

"What's that?" Gerard asked.

"His son got into a lot of trouble," Jax said.

"Now you're right there," Griffin agreed, looking further at the folder, nodding. "It's quite possible that Bram here has been compromised. I'd hate to think it though."

"What about his son?" Gerard asked.

"He was caught with a dead woman. Somebody's daughter from Saudi Arabia," Griffin said. "They were doing drugs at the time."

Gerard nodded. "Bram told me about that, as soon as it was discovered. So, not only were drugs not allowed in that area," Gerard said, "but the fact that she died would also have caused quite a kerfuffle. Still, I thought that was settled."

"Regardless, it gives Bram a weakness someone could exploit," Griffin added.

"And, of course, we must remember that just because it could have happened doesn't mean it did happen," Gerard noted.

"Exactly," Jax said.

"Is he around? Can we talk to him?" Griffin asked.

Gerard picked up the phone and made a call. Within ten minutes, they could hear footsteps walking down the hallway. Bram stepped in a side door, nodded at Gerard, and said, "What can I do for you?"

Gerard motioned to the two men standing just behind Bram.

"Well, well, well. Jax and Griffin. Who knew? You guys are like bad pennies," Bram said, smiling.

"Meaning, we show up where we're not wanted?" Griffin asked drily. His comment was certainly appropriate given the fact that Bram was the one being investigated first.

"Absolutely," Glenn Bram said. "And, if you're here, it means something's going on that I currently don't know about."

Griffin nodded and said, "Well, we have some good news but also some bad news."

"The girls," Bram froze. "Did you hear from the kidnapper?"

"No," said a voice from the doorway. Amelia Rose and Lorelei stepped in.

Bram's face broke out into a huge smile. Griffin had been watching, and that man in front of them was overjoyed at their safe rescue. That was huge for Griffin. He looked at Jax, and his partner nodded, whereas Bram held his arms open and Amelia Rose raced into them.

"You got them back," Bram said, when he finally could, his voice breaking slightly. As soon as Amelia Rose had stepped out of his arms, he turned to face Griffin and Jax. "Well, now I know why you guys are here. That's definitely your kind of a job." He turned toward Gerard. "I don't know how you found these guys, but these men are the best."

Gerard's face worked with emotion as he nodded and said, "And they did get Amelia Rose back. Lorelei as well."

"Nurse?"

At that, grief crossed Gerard's features, and he took a moment before he could answer. "They killed her," he said, "as a way to get Lorelei's and Amelia Rose's cooperation. My girls escaped and went looking for help, then were recaptured and Nurse killed, as a threat of what would happen to them if they tried to escape again."

"And yet," Griffin stepped in to say immediately, "that wasn't their fault."

Bram nodded. "Exactly. It doesn't mean the killing wouldn't have happened anyway. There's no real way to know with guys like that." He looked at the two men. "Did you take out the kidnappers?"

Both men shook their heads. "That's partly why we're here now," Griffin said.

Bram's features sharpened. "You think he's from home soil?"

Griffin hesitated, glanced at Gerard, and then said, "Unfortunately I think it's closer than home soil. I think it's a home job. Meaning ..."

Bram's back stiffened. There was no doubt that he understood the implication.

"We think it's somebody in the family," Jax filled in immediately. "At least one," he murmured.

But instead of showing any surprise, Bram nodded. "Sorry, Gerard, but I've been wondering about that ever since the kidnapping. But I don't have any reason to look at anyone in particular." Bram held up his hand to quiet Gerard.

Oddly enough Gerard did as asked.

"Hear me out this time," Bram began. "It's just too convenient how everyone's alibis are all nicely locked down as everyone was here. Yet someone is pulling the strings from a distance. Still, that means there are too many possible suspects, and they are all connected to you, Gerard, and the massive corporate network you've built. Requires someone in the know. Someone who could contract men in Thailand. Which brings it back to your sons, your wife, and your brother. Wendy much less so because she is never involved in the businesses, but, with her proclivity for men in her bed, … it's possible."

"And yet, you didn't tell me?" Gerard asked in shock.

Bram faced him with a grimace. "The one thing about you is, I have to come with hard evidence for you to listen. Otherwise nobody gets to say anything about family."

Gerard had the grace to look ashamed, and Griffin understood. After all, he and Jax had pretty well been kicked out of the house themselves for having said or implied something along that same line.

"And I hate to say it," Jax said, "but one of the first people we have to start with—and, of course, we want to completely clear—is the head of security."

Bram nodded. "And that's to be expected. So what do you want to know?"

"Has somebody been blackmailing you or asking you for information that they shouldn't be or contacting you in any way, shape, or form that they shouldn't have?" Griffin asked Bram. "You know the drill."

"I do," he said. "And you're thinking about my son and his troubles, aren't you?"

"Yes," Griffin said instantly. "I am. Obviously that situation is one that we wished hadn't happened in the first place, but it does leave you open as those doors weren't permanently closed."

"And, if they had been permanently closed," Bram said, "then I would be in even more trouble."

"To a certain extent, yes. That's definitely a possibility."

"First let me say ..." He nodded at Gerard. "I told Gerard as soon as I found out and have been upfront and honest with him thereafter, keeping him updated." Then Bram addressed all of them. "Well, my son was cleared of all wrongdoing," Bram said. "He's currently in drug rehab and has been for the past three months. It's too early to tell if it'll work this go-round or not. It's not the first time we've had him there. I keep hoping each and every time that it will be the last, but I'm not a fool. I know that, chances are, it won't be his final stint in rehab." There was such sadness in his expression that Griffin didn't get any sense of betrayal from him.

"So nobody's tried to blackmail you or compromise your position here?" Griffin asked for clarity. He wanted Bram to look him in the eye and tell him no. And that's what Bram did.

He looked him in the eye and said, "No, none."

Griffin nodded. "And you have responsibility for hiring all the security for the company and the family?"

At that, Bram looked surprised. He shook his head. "Absolutely not. I'm not sure where you got that idea from."

Griffin looked at Gerard. "Gerard?"

He stared at Bram. "Of course you do."

Bram shook his head. "No, I used to, until that was taken away, and other people hired their own people."

"Who took that away?" Gerard asked in shock. "Who's

usurping my authority?"

Unfortunately Bram just looked at Gerard quietly and said, "I think it's everybody."

Gerard stared at him, completely flabbergasted, and Bram explained. "Remember how your son wanted one of his childhood friends on staff? And the only place that he was in any way qualified was as security. That started it. Then your wife wanted somebody also hired, and again the only place for that person was in security. Even your brother has had his hand in making sure he had somebody on security. And all of that because they wanted to know that somebody was looking after *them* and their interests."

Jax asked slowly, "Is that what's going on here, Bram?"

"I'm not sure if it's that or the fact that, as soon as one manages to wrestle a little bit of control away from Gerard, everybody else tries to as well."

Griffin looked at Jax, and then the two of them faced Gerard. "Did you realize that this has been happening?"

His face worked into a grimace, and he stared at Bram. "I remember them fighting over it, and me telling you it didn't matter."

At that, Bram gave a decisive nod and said, "Exactly. And, once that happened, other people got hired on. There are friends who work in the household staff, and there are *acquaintances* ..." He said that part and the next with emphasis. "... who *work* on the grounds ..." And he let his voice trail off.

Griffin pulled out the list he'd gotten from Lorelei and Amelia Rose and said, "Do you have any of those names?"

"John Halffinger works in the stables," he said instantly. Then he stopped and looked at Gerard. "A friend of your wife's."

Gerard winced. "I'm paying this guy to shag my wife?"

That got a laugh out of Bram. It was totally inappropriate with Amelia Rose here, but at least Gerard had a sense of humor. Griffin looked to see Lorelei standing beside Jax with Amelia Rose. But then the girls had given them the name of Amelia Rose's mother's lover, so obviously not too many secrets were here.

"And who else?" Jax asked, leaning over so he could look at the list that the girls had given them.

Bram proceeded to name four others on that list.

Gerard shook his head. "I don't even know those names."

"One is on the cooking staff in the kitchen," he said. "It's one of your sons' school friends."

Gerard frowned, remembering that, and then dismissing it. "I'm sure that was somebody he went to school with. What's the problem with that?" A heavy pause ensued as Gerard looked from one to the others around him. "He's in the kitchen, for God's sake."

Lorelei stepped forward and said, "What a perfect place to poison somebody or to kill somebody through allergies."

Gerard just stared at her, his face settling into hard lines. "I'll say it once more. I really hate this, but it's a shitty world we live in."

They went through each and every name that Bram came up with, and then they started in with the actual security people he was responsible for, and the six he hadn't approved who were assigned to other members of the family even though Gerard signed their paychecks. By the time they were done, Gerard was almost gray-faced. "So is there anybody I hired and am paying for who is loyal to me?"

Bram immediately nodded and said, "The men I've

hired who are on staff here specifically to look after you," he said. "As long as I can keep them around, then we can do the job that needs to be done."

"*If you can keep them around?* What does that mean?" Griffin asked.

Bram looked at Gerard and said, "I hate to bring this up again, but your sons often take security away from you when the boys take trips, and often you just don't seem to care."

"Well, because keeping my sons safe is paramount," he said. "That's not the same thing."

"Well, it is," Jax said, "if they're behind any of this."

"And if they want you less guarded while they set up an attack on you personally," Griffin added.

And once again Gerard's face stilled. His big shoulders sagged as he slumped into his chair. "So now what?"

"We compile everybody's movements at least two weeks prior to the girls' first kidnapping event," Griffin said immediately. "We need to know exactly where everybody was and who was on what duty." He looked at Bram. "How many of these questionable men might have had anything to do with this ransom drop where nobody showed up?"

Bram looked at him in surprise and then nodded. "Good point," he said. "Only mine were hired to run the ransom drop and to protect Gerard here, but that then left a lot of the other men to be present for the other side."

"But nobody showed up on the other side," Gerard said in exasperation.

"I know," Griffin said. "And how much of that was because they already had insider information that the money was fake and that the drop was a MI6 trap?" There was silence in the room, and then finally Griffin said, "Look. We can talk until we're blue in the face, but we need to clear

Bram here, and Bram needs to help us go through every staff member on this estate, not just security, and see who might be aiding and abetting that kidnapping."

"If it's anybody on my staff," Gerard said, "I want them fired, and I want them legally charged."

"All fine and dandy," Bram said. "We still have to find out who they are first."

"We'll do a close review of all staff, but we're starting with the security personnel," Griffin stated.

And, at that, they were given a room with computers and areas to interview staff. They compiled a complete rundown on who had been available, who was off doing other work, and what the relationships were between the various staff. When Griffin began the face-to-face interviews, meeting Bram's security guards, they stood out. It wasn't just the look of them, but they were well-trained, used to obeying orders, and understood security from the inside out.

The friends who had been brought in to specifically serve the other family members were a completely different group of security personnel. Not that they were involved in criminal activity in any outward way, but they definitely weren't of the same ilk. They were completely uncomfortable with being questioned. They didn't stand in any neutral position. They looked guilty right from the get-go, most likely because they already knew that they weren't right for those jobs. They hadn't trained for them. They weren't experienced. They had nothing real to offer for a position such as this one.

And yet, they were all taking Gerard's money. Maybe they were learning something, and maybe they were grateful for the opportunity and were doing their best. Griffin would like to think some were. Two of them though, he highly doubted. As soon as both of those men left, Griffin looked at Gerard, snorted, and said, "Seriously?"

He winced and said, "My wife's suggestions."

Griffin jotted that down. His wife obviously had a predilection to young, brawny, and potentially nothing-between-the-ears stud material. Even Lorelei, who'd come and gone several times, smirked as she walked in, crossing paths as one of those men walked out.

"Do you know those last two men?" he asked her.

"Sure, insofar as they showed up one day with jobs," she said cheerfully.

"Did you ever see them working?"

Her tone was completely bland as she said with twinkling eyes, "Tell me what their job was, and I might be able to answer you."

Gerard snapped at her. "I get that this is funny to you, but it's not funny to me."

Immediately her face sobered. She nodded and said, "So, therefore, to be direct, I highly doubt I've seen them doing anything that you would be paying them for."

He glared at her, then groaned and said, "Really? That pair too?"

She nodded. "Yes. That pair too."

"Please tell me that my daughter didn't see them ... together."

"Not that last one," Amelia Rose said. "Just the two in the barn and the gardener."

Her father stared at her in horror.

She shrugged and said, "Living here is an education too. Into human relationships. How to treat people, whether family, friends, or coworkers." She giggled. "Besides, Poppy, your business is to write all about the news. Well, at least some of your businesses do that. So Lorelei said I should research my poppy's company of companies to figure out what I want to do with my life. To figure out where I would best fit in, where I would enjoy my work. Right, Lorelei?" On that, she smirked and walked out.

Gerard sat there, clearly overwhelmed. "When did eleven-year-olds become so worldly?"

Griffin wisely stayed quiet. So did Jax.

Bram, on the other hand, said, "She's still probably better off being more worldly and wise than vulnerable through blind innocence."

Gerard nodded, yet said, "Still way too young."

"Maybe," Griffin said, "but I don't think *young* means *naive* anymore."

Gerard studied him for a long moment, sighed, and said, "Back to work. And then I'll take steps to stop being the laughingstock of my own household," he growled.

Lorelei shook her head. "You're not the laughingstock," she said. "Your wife is."

He looked at her and said, "But I'm being conned."

"Sure, but you're allowing your wife's dalliances, and you don't care. That's the difference. She thinks she's deceiving everybody, yet nobody is unaware of her affairs. That changes others' perceptions entirely."

"Thank you. I'll take that as a small salve to my conscience," he said.

She chuckled. "You know something has to be done about it, other than firing her lovers. When you're ready, you'll do it."

"What am I to do about Wendy? She's Amelia Rose's mother," he growled.

"While you certainly have grounds for a divorce," Lorelei

said, proving that once again she had a unique position in the household, "it's all up to you to do whatever you feel is right."

"If anything," he said, "I was hoping my daughter would get a little older first."

"She clearly is old enough to understand too much now," Lorelei said gently. "You can hear it in her words alone. Keeping this marriage going for her sake is more about teaching her that marital vows have no meaning. Of course that's a very British way to look at things. It's supposed to be the heir and the spare, but you already had those to begin with, so there really are no rules to wealthy British marriages now, are there?"

He snorted and said, "That's one way to look at it. Not the easiest and not the nicest but the old way. Yet the fact that Wendy's a tramp doesn't mean that she's done anything criminal. I still refuse to believe that she would do anything to hurt her daughter."

"Quite possibly," Griffin said, "but is there anything she's done that would put her in a position of being compromised?"

Jax snorted. "Sounds like the much harder question would be finding things she's done where she wasn't compromised."

They all sat here for a moment in silence, thinking about the woman with the blatant disregard for her husband's reputation and who had complete disregard for her daughter's well-being.

"The thing is, it would have to be something *so* major," Lorelei said, "for Wendy to even care about any repercussions from her actions."

"She's not likely done anything like that," Gerard said

heavily. "She cares about studs, two- and four-legged ones. When we found out she was pregnant, I was ecstatic—she was not. She wanted an abortion or an open marriage. It was no contest to me. She's no different now than when I first met her. I just can't keep living like this. And I can't keep putting Amelia Rose in these unhealthy situations."

CHAPTER 12

L ISTENING TO THE men discuss the issues was fascinating. Lorelei wasn't sure how she'd been allowed to stay as a party to this except for the list that she had created with Amelia Rose's assistance. Amelia Rose had taken off to play, as they certainly didn't have any school lessons scheduled for right now while they both recuperated from their ordeal. When lunch had been served, Lorelei sat beside Griffin. And, when the day was finally done, she looked at the two men and said, "Does that give you any answers?"

Bram answered, "More to the point, it narrowed the field. We have everybody in a security position cleared except for two."

"Which two?" she asked. "And were they not cleared just because they aren't here?" The men shrugged but didn't offer more information. "And what about the family?"

"Family is the next layer," Bram said. "We have to know who we can trust before we start combating the war that's being waged from within."

"Do you think it was insidious intent or is this all by accident, this salting of unqualified men within the actual family members?" Lorelei asked. "Are they just circumstantial and random hires? Because you know now that hand-picked people are inside the house. More hand-picked people are inside the kitchen, even in the other security team, for

God's sake. Therefore, all facets of Gerard's working life here from home are handled by people who were hired by somebody other than himself."

Griffin looked at her and smiled. "Figured that out, did you?"

She nodded, a sad expression on her face.

"I'm not sure how this plays out though," Bram said. "That's what we're still figuring out."

Gerard growled and looked at Lorelei. "Where's Amelia Rose?"

"She's in her room, playing computer games."

"Could you please check?"

"I can." She didn't worry about Amelia Rose in her own home before, but, as they looked at the problems Gerard had with the household staffing, it would certainly be something Lorelei considered moving forward. With them doing this investigation, it would just bring up even more issues of trust for Amelia Rose among the staff. Lorelei pulled out her phone and called her charge.

Amelia Rose immediately answered the landline in her bedroom. "Yes, I'm here. Yes, I'm fine and exactly the same since the last ten minutes when you contacted me."

Lorelei chuckled. "It was an hour ago, and your father asked me to check this time."

Lorelei raised her voice and said, "Poppy, I'm fine."

"Good," he grumbled. "But you didn't come for food."

"I ate earlier," she said. "And I'm going to bed early too. I'm really tired." And her voice did sound pretty rough.

Lorelei took that as a hint and said to the girl, "I'm on my way up."

"Thank you," Amelia Rose said, her words filled with obvious relief as she spoke.

When Amelia Rose hung up, Lorelei looked at Gerard and said, "It'll take her a while to settle down and to know that she isn't in danger anymore."

"And, for that," her father said, "we'll keep working on getting to the bottom of this from our end. But please, Bram, make sure my daughter is safe, particularly while she sleeps in her own bed."

"I'll post a man at her door right now," Bram said.

Lorelei winced. "That's not guaranteed to make any of us sleep well tonight."

"I know," Gerard said. "But this first gambit's been tossed, and the kidnappers lost. I mean, it would make sense for them to try it again, from home now."

"Well, I hope you're wrong," she said. "It's not what I want to consider at all."

He nodded. "I'll be up to say good night to my daughter in a little bit. Tell her that, will you?"

She nodded. "You know that she does understand that you do love her and that you will do anything to keep her safe."

Gerard smiled. "Thank you for that. She's very important to me."

"All your children are," Lorelei said. "I hope they all know it."

"I do too," he said as he stared down at the list. "God, I hope so."

NOT LONG AFTER Lorelei left, the men wrapped it up. Gerard's sons were both coming for a meeting the next morning, both of them perturbed at the call from Gerard's home to theirs. And Gerard's wife, who apparently was still out of town, would return as well. Gerard was determined to get to the bottom of this and have face-to-face meetings with everyone. Griffin didn't have a problem with that. He just knew that those kinds of meetings rarely turned out the way people expected them to. But, hey, good luck to Gerard.

Griffin was shown to a first-floor guest room not long afterward, with Jax in the guest room next door. As Griffin got ready for bed, he checked his watch. *Already one in the morning.* Somehow their entire Thursday had disappeared. Then that tended to happen on these jobs. That's what he was used to, but he couldn't get Lorelei off his mind.

He'd slept beside her for the last several nights, if only for her own comfort, but he found that he was used to it himself, and he wanted to continue sleeping beside her. Walking away from that tonight was hard, and it would likely be every night from now on too. He walked into his en suite bathroom, closed the door, and had a quick shower. When he came out, he felt a deep sense of unease. And instinctively he knew Lorelei was suffering. He sat down, pulled out his phone, and texted her. **You okay?**

There was a delayed response, which, for a moment, he thought meant that she was sound asleep, and then she texted back. **How did you know?**

Instinct. I just got out of a shower, and it felt wrong. If we were anywhere close, I would have automatically come to see if you were okay. As it is, a text is about all I can do.

I have to get used to sleeping alone. I can't depend on you to chase away the boogeymen.

No, he typed in. **But I'm sorry if you're not getting any sleep. How was Amelia Rose?**

She seems to be sleeping fine came the response.

Wish I could.

He understood. **Well, I can't walk through the halls of this place easily. I don't even know where your room is. But you can always come visit me.**

And he left it hanging of course. For all he knew, she'd lose her job if she did come to him. And he didn't want to put that on her either. Knowing that there was probably no way for them to be together under Gerard's roof, Griffin got into bed and closed his eyes. When his door opened ten minutes later, he was already alert and watching.

She poked her head around the corner and stepped in. He didn't say a word. He just pulled back the blankets, and she crawled in. With a heavy sigh, she rolled over, backed up against him, and fell asleep.

He whispered against her hair, "This is really a bad habit."

He thought she was out cold, but she responded. "I know, but I figured there'll be lots of times to learn to adjust, and I shouldn't have to do it tonight." And, with that, she shuffled closer, and this time she did fall asleep.

He laid here with her in his arms for a long time. He needed sleep too, but this bundle of crazy comfort that he himself gained from holding her made him realize just how important she was to him. That in itself wouldn't be easy to handle. It was pretty damn hard to have a relationship, given their professions. And, even if they did get that far, it's not like he would be changing his. Although this was supposed to be a one-time deal, and he was already on a second Mavericks op, so he didn't know how that would work out long-term.

He laid here for a long moment and then thought he heard something. He froze, not wanting to disturb Lorelei, and, when a text beep came through, he reached for his phone.

Are you there? Jax asked.

Yeah, he replied. **Heard something out in the hall. Don't know if Lorelei was followed.** That was something he hadn't considered, and maybe he should have with everything going on. This wasn't likely the best idea they'd had.

Jax sent back a smiley face, then added, **I'll check it out.**

Griffin heard just the hint of a sound from his partner's bedroom, but, even then, he knew something was off about this whole thing. Never, at any point in time, had he considered that Lorelei might have been an inciting party to this kidnapping, working with whoever else had planned this fiasco. And he sure as hell would hate to think of it now because it would mean his instincts were completely off, but he had to wonder.

And then he realized, no, it just wasn't part of who she was, no matter how people might look at this. No one understood how hard it was to get over a kidnapping. Besides, she'd had lots of opportunities to take him or Jax out. And she had done nothing but protect Amelia Rose.

When he heard something again outside, he gently stepped out of bed, made sure that she didn't rouse from his movements, and texted Jax. When Griffin got no reply, he went to the door and listened. He heard something. *A scuffle.*

He opened the door silently and stuck his head out. Somebody came out of nowhere and smacked him hard on his jaw. He went down but was already rolling to come back up again. He lashed out with his foot, catching his assailant, dropping him hard on the floor beside him. He continued to fight hard and fast, and he caught sight of Jax's fight going on beside him.

But the thought uppermost in Griffin's mind was that Lorelei was here. Hopefully she was sound asleep. But what if she wasn't? He hated the dangling suspicion that said, what if she was behind this attack? He knew it couldn't be true, but, until he got to the bottom of this, he had willingly forgone taking a closer look at her.

And just when he took another blow and a hard boot to a rib, he heard a loud crash. He turned to see his assailant dropping. Lorelei stood trembling in the doorway with a lamp in her hand. The glass had been shattered over his assailant's head. Well, that answered that question. He bounced to his feet, kissed her hard, and whispered, "Thank you. Now go inside and lock the door." And he shut the door in her face.

He then went after Jax's attacker. Within minutes, he had him subdued and tied up beside the other one. "Those two men we haven't interviewed," he said.

"I know," Jax said, gasping, bent over, regaining his breath. "So, are they the missing two, or are they part of some completely different group that is involved?"

"This is getting ridiculous," Griffin said. He pulled out his phone and phoned Gerard.

A sleepy voice answered.

"This is Griffin. Two assailants attacked Jax and me. We have them both tied up in the hallway. What do you want to do?"

Gerard became fully awake. Immediately he roared, "What? In my own house?"

"We need to check on Amelia Rose."

Gerard was already up and running. "I'm racing toward her bedroom right now. I don't know who else they would be after."

"Well, they came after us," Griffin said, "but I'm not sure why."

"It has to be the investigations into my staff," Gerard said over the phone.

"Maybe," Griffin said, still thinking it through.

Griffin could hear Gerard speaking to the guard before opening the door and then the relief in his voice when he said, "Amelia Rose is in bed, sound asleep."

"Thank heavens for that." He gave Jax a thumbs-up.

"I'll wake Lorelei and bring her here."

"Don't worry about it," Griffin said. "I'll send her up."

An edgy silence followed on the other end as Gerard assimilated that information. But his voice was hard when he said, "You do that, and then we'll talk."

Just then Lorelei stepped through the doorway, listening from the other side. She reached out for Griffin's phone. "There's nothing to talk about," she said in a cool tone to Gerard. "I can't sleep since the kidnapping. I'm the one who came down to Griffin. And these two intruders may have followed me. I don't know. But both have been secured, and I don't recognize either of them."

"You come up here to Amelia Rose," Gerard said, his tone back to normal. "I'm coming there. Maybe I'll know them."

As Lorelei raced past them, Jax punched Griffin lightly in the shoulder. "Nice woman," he said, "especially when she stands up and defends you."

"That *is* why she came down here," Griffin said with a wry smile. "She hasn't slept since."

"And we both understand that," Jax said. "Still doesn't change the fact that there's something between you guys."

"Sure, but what?"

"Well, it's not like either of you are involved with anyone else. So there's nothing really stopping you from having a relationship."

"Just our jobs," Griffin said with a note of laughter.

"Yeah, well, there is that. Not sure that we are even full-time with the Mavericks much less that we know what we're doing with our futures now, do we?"

"I thought the Mavericks gig was temporary," Griffin said. "But I thought that when I helped out Kerrick. That's when I was called into play. Now I'm not sure what the deal is. Except this seems almost like an initiation."

"The Mavericks team is not for everyone," Jax said. "Yet I think a lot of navy guys, those with families, end up leaving the navy before they really want to. And this Mavericks life might work better for them. Or maybe those family guys just wanted the navy to change some of its rules."

"Hell, I'm single, and I was ready to leave before they tagged me for this job," Griffin said. "I just hadn't figured out what I would do in the meantime."

"Well, figure it out, and, if they need to tag you for jobs like this, that's an option too," he said. "Nobody said it had to be permanent and forever with the Mavericks."

"I know. Just feels odd."

"That's because this op got to you. Because it's been a while since you had a real relationship," Jax said. "It hurts you when someone you care about gets hurt."

"Absolutely it does." Gerard barged into the hallway, having obviously heard part of their conversation. "And if there's anything there worth keeping, then you fight for it. But I really won't take kindly to you playing fast and loose with Lorelei, and she'd have my head if I were to say that in her hearing."

"She would, indeed," Griffin said. "And I don't know what's going on between us. So far, it's been a case of comfort." He let them know quite clearly that they hadn't crossed that line. But it showed how he wanted to.

"Well, it won't be for long," Gerard said. "She's a hell of a good woman, and I really don't want to think of her getting hurt."

"Well, you're a little late for that," Griffin said, glaring at him. "She got hurt on this trip."

"That's why I'm trying to stop it from happening again," Gerard roared.

Griffin motioned to the two men on the ground. "Who the hell are these guys?"

One was conscious, a T-shirt of Griffin's stuck in his mouth; the other was still out cold. Griffin rolled the one out cold over so that Gerard could see his face too. He stared at them in shock. "They both work for me. These are the two security men who we never got around to interviewing because we couldn't find them."

"Who hired them?"

"My brother," he said, frowning. "But that doesn't mean he knew these guys would turn against me."

"No, not at all," Griffin said. "As we know, men are turned all the time. These bad guys prey on that chance."

The two men were lifted and hauled to Gerard's office, and Bram was woken up and brought down to deal with the pair. When he recognized them, his face thinned, and his jaw firmed. He frowned at Gerard, pointed to one, and said, "This is the one I fought against being hired."

"And I overruled you, I suppose," Gerard said, sagging into his oversize leather chair.

Bram nodded. "That you did. Your brother wanted this one brought in and trained, and why was that?"

"I don't know," he said. "Son of a friend of his or some such bullshit."

"Well, we need to know exactly what that was all about," Griffin stated firmly, "because now, apparently, it's a bigger issue than it was before."

"It is, indeed," Bram said. "It is, indeed."

Very quickly Gerard's brother, Joe, was ordered to attend the meeting that morning with Gerard's sons. Groggy from being woken up, Joe said, "I'll be there in a few hours."

Gerard interrupted. "Don't bother. I'm sending the chopper now."

"This must be important," Joe said.

"It is," he said. "I'm calling a family meeting." And he proceeded to wake up the rest of his family, ordering them all to attend earlier than planned.

Griffin had asked that Gerard make the calls with speaker engaged, so Griffin heard a lot of groaning and bitching on the other end of the calls, but nobody flat-out said no. Gerard was the money and the power behind the company and the ultimate head of the family hierarchy. When he said jump, they all jumped. But it was easy for Griffin to see that some of them were very tired of jumping.

When he hung up the phone, Gerard stared at it for a long time. "A lot of dissent is all around, isn't it?"

"It could very well be too tight a glove on some of them for too long," Griffin said boldly. "Everybody starts to chafe after a while."

"So what's the answer? I'm not ready to retire."

"Bring them in more," Jax said. "Give them more responsibility, and give them a bigger role in running the company."

"They already are though."

Bram made an odd sound.

Gerard looked at him and asked, "Aren't they?"

Bram shrugged. "Not as much as they'd like to be. You do keep them fairly tightly held."

"Well, that's because I'm not ready to hand over control of the company," he snapped.

"Of course not," Bram said. "But then you have to expect that people want more, want to move up the ladder. And when they want more for a long time, they eventually do something about getting more. So you should listen more closely to what they say. Pick up on these disgruntled moments. Allow people to be honest with you, to share a different opinion. Your sons are capable businessmen in their own right. Your brother has been with you since the beginning. Hell, your father started this company, and you two inherited; but you made it massive, and Joe's been left in a supporting role all this time. That, however, doesn't mean that any of them are behind the kidnapping or this latest assault."

"Have your security feeds been checked?" Jax asked. "Do we know if any other men came onto the grounds overnight?"

"Not that I've seen," Bram said. "I've got two men looking right now." Just then his phone rang. He answered it, frowned, and said, "Make sure you've got a full coalition of men. I want all four of them brought into Gerard's office." He put away his phone and said, "They found two others outside and have a line on two more at the stables."

"Six men?" Gerard asked. "What the hell?"

Bram nodded. "Six. What we're trying to do is make

sure we catch them all right now. So we can finally get to the bottom of this."

"Do you have enough men?" Jax asked. "We can help."

"We're good," Bram said, "and my security team has been fully warned after all the interviews yesterday that something was up."

"Right, so make sure only men who were cleared yesterday are on this," Gerard snapped.

Griffin, already feeling like something else was going on, said, "I don't like it. It still feels like distractions."

"From what?"

"I don't know," he said, "but I don't like it." He pulled out his phone and quickly phoned Lorelei. There was no answer. He bolted to his feet and said, "Where's Amelia Rose's room? I don't like this."

Gerard looked at him, already standing, and asked, "Did you contact Lorelei?"

"Yes, and there's no answer."

"Let's go," Gerard said.

Jax stood guard on the prisoners with Bram while Griffin and Gerard raced up to Lorelei's room. Before they got there, Griffin already knew they would be too late. Gerard bolted into his daughter's room and froze. Her bed was empty, the guard out cold down the hall, and there was no sign of either of the girls. He turned in horror to look at Griffin. "What the hell?"

Griffin didn't bother answering—he was already heading downstairs and outside.

CHAPTER 13

LORELEI WOKE TO a pounding headache. It didn't take long to realize that she'd been knocked out and taken prisoner by somebody. That she had been walking into Amelia Rose's room at the time terrified her even more. Where was Amelia Rose? She desperately tried to stay quiet as she rolled over, searching for her, but the pain almost blacked her out. When she could control her breathing enough to control her pain, she opened her eyes, found Amelia Rose lying beside her.

Her eyes were wide open, and she had a finger to her lips.

Grateful that she was unhurt, Lorelei sank back down and tried hard to get her brain to function again. She could hear voices outside, but the smell told her where she was. At least where she hoped she was.

They were in the stables.

Hay, sweat, and manure filled her nostrils. Surely somebody in the house would notice. Gerard was already well aware of the attack on Griffin and Jax, meaning that she and Amelia Rose should be found soon enough.

Amelia Rose's gaze was terrified as she gently rubbed Lorelei's face, but she didn't say anything.

Lorelei didn't know if the child wasn't speaking because they weren't alone, which was possible, or because she was too shocked to say anything. Lorelei captured her finger and held on. Either way, it was not good.

As she waited for her headache to ease back, Lorelei took stock. She wasn't tied up or restrained in any way, which meant either they were under guard or they were in a locked room. As she looked around, she recognized the horse tack room, confirming that they were, indeed, still on the property. That made her feel much better. She knew where she was, and she wasn't too far away from Griffin.

And, at least for now, Amelia Rose was okay—but not for long. The voices were loud, irate, and close to her. She didn't really recognize any of them though. She rolled over ever-so-softly. The tack room had half doors, and the people arguing were just outside, so it's not like she and Amelia Rose had any way to leave without being seen. That explained why Amelia Rose wasn't talking. Lorelei quickly checked her pocket, found her phone, and sent Griffin a text. **Tack room, stable one.**

Then she slipped her cell back into her pocket, held her finger up to Amelia Rose's lips, and whispered, "Griffin."

Immediately Amelia Rose's eyes grew wide, and she nodded. Hope entered her gaze as she realized that maybe, just maybe, a rescue was coming.

Lorelei lay here, quiet, trying to discern the voices and how far away they were, as she took stock of their options. She needed a weapon, any weapon. The bedroom lamp had done a hell of a job, so what could she use in here? There were bridles and bits, both which, when swung with a hefty motion, would give a hell of a blow. But, if she moved, somebody was likely to know that she was awake. She studied one of the bits hanging on the wall and motioned at it with her head. Amelia Rose followed her gaze, saw the bit, and frowned. Lorelei whispered, "Weapon."

Almost immediately Amelia Rose understood; she snagged the bit off the wall and came back beside Lorelei. The bit was attached to a metal lead. She separated the two so that they each had a weapon, one a little less effective than the other, and, when she heard footsteps, quickly laid on top of both of them, back into the same position, and closed her eyes.

"The oldest one's still out," one of the men said. "How hard did you hit her?"

"Not hard," somebody said.

At that, the man walked away again.

"What about the kid? Is she still asleep?"

"They both look it," he said without much care. "As far as I'm concerned, it's easier if we just kill them now."

"No killing," a sharp voice came from the far side. "We agreed, no killing."

There was something about that tone. The voice had been partially disguised, but it was almost identifiable. Lorelei frowned, thinking about it, but it was hard to focus, not to mention her brain still felt scrambled. She didn't know how long it would take for Griffin to set up a plan. What she didn't want was for them to get caught too. No point in trying to rescue the two of them if they all ended up captured. She pulled out her phone and sent yet another text. **Hurry.**

This time she got a response. **Almost there.**

She held it up for Amelia Rose to see. She smiled and hunkered down closer to Lorelei. The two of them just lay here, waiting and knowing that the attack would come when they least expected it, and they wanted to be ready to take advantage of any opportunity they could. When it happened, it was even more of a surprise because it came from the other end of the stable.

They heard voices, then grunting and sounds of a fight, and then, just like that, Griffin opened the stall door and raced into the room beside them. Gerard was right behind him. He reached for Amelia Rose and hugged her close, whereas Griffin grabbed Lorelei and just held her tight. She cuddled in closer and said, "See? I told you that we shouldn't be apart."

He laughed. "You didn't say anything about that."

"Maybe not," she said, "but I'm saying that now. This is ridiculous every damn time, and who was it this time?"

"Unfortunately it was the same as the last time," Gerard said, his tone thick with emotion.

Only Lorelei didn't have a clue. "Why are we in the barn?" she asked. "Wouldn't it have been smarter to take us immediately off the property?"

"Well, that was in progress," Gerard said. "But who do you know who spends so much time in the barn?"

She looked at him in horror. "Surely not Wendy?"

Gerard nodded ever-so-slowly. "Yes, Amelia Rose's mother. But we have no proof yet."

"Or it was made to look like she'd be the guilty party?" Lorelei suggested, hoping for the best.

Griffin didn't say anything. Lorelei looked to him for confirmation, but a thoughtful look passed his face. She nudged him. "Is that your take too?"

"Partly," he said. "I'm not sure if that's all of it though."

Gerard looked at him in shock. "What are you saying?"

"Not sure yet," he said. "But how about we get the girls back to the house and take our prisoners in for a little interrogation?"

Gerard snorted. "How about we just deep-six them all?"

"Can't get answers off a dead man," he said, "or a dead woman, for that matter."

Trying to stand wasn't easy. Lorelei's legs were still a little bit goofy. She looked up at Griffin, his arms around her, and she said, "You know that it'll be almost impossible to sleep now, right?"

He just smiled and didn't say anything.

She sighed. "I guess I'll have to get used to it though."

"You would anyway," he said. "I still have a job."

"True," she said. "I couldn't possibly be with somebody who was unemployed."

He chuckled. "Is that what we are, somebody with somebody?"

"Hell no," she said. "I'd never sleep alone again if I had a choice."

"Well, I'm hardly just a replacement for a teddy bear," he said smoothly.

"Well, you're very teddy-bear-like, but you make a hell of a better protector."

"What kind of a protector was I? You were kidnapped yet again."

"I wondered for a moment there if that was Gerard's doing."

Gerard looked at her and said, "What?"

"Well, you're the one who sent me to Amelia Rose's room."

"Sure, to keep her safe," he said in outrage. "I wasn't expecting my own wife to be finagling her daughter's kidnapping."

"Well, did you start divorce proceedings?"

He flushed. "I'm thinking about it, but I haven't done

anything officially."

"Well," Griffin added, "somewhere along the line, she got wind of her future, and, before she would let you have Amelia Rose, Wendy decided she would take her daughter and enough money to make sure *Wendy* would be okay. … I'm not sure if that money was for Amelia Rose too, but most likely it was because the child makes a good bargaining chip later on too."

As the solemn group made their way back to the house, vehicles arrived.

Lorelei glanced at Griffin and asked, "What's this all about?"

"Gerard called a family meeting to get to the bottom of this," he said. "And this is him sending out the word and ordering everybody to show up."

"Right, and Wendy was supposed to as well, wasn't she? I thought someone said she was out of town."

"I'm pretty sure she was already here," Griffon said. They walked into Gerard's adjoining offices, which had been opened to make it more of a boardroom. Griffin approved of everybody being in one spot.

With Bram running security, the prisoners were all led in; Lorelei and Amelia Rose stayed in the hallway, and Gerard's sons gasped, "What on earth, Father?"

"Amelia Rose, Lorelei, and Nurse," Gerard said with great difficulty, "were just in Thailand for a holiday."

"Right. And were kidnapped. We know all that. Are these the men responsible?" asked one of his sons.

"Yes," he said.

"Is Amelia Rose okay?" asked his other son.

Gerard nodded. "I can't tell you what kind of a nightmare I've been through dealing with this."

Amelia Rose and Lorelei stepped inside.

His sons stared at Gerard, then turned to look at Lorelei and Amelia Rose.

Lorelei nodded and said, "Yes, we are safe. We only got home a few hours ago."

"You didn't tell us she was safe," his eldest son protested, staring at Gerard, anger deepening the lines on his face. "Why didn't you tell us? Amelia Rose is our sister too."

"I did tell you that we did a ransom drop, and nobody came to pick it up. It was all very hush-hush. Instead, these men"—he motioned at Jax and Griffin—"rescued both of them in Thailand and returned them here to me."

"And Nurse?" one of the sons asked, looking around. "Is she in bed?"

"She was murdered in Thailand," Gerard said in a heavy voice. "Her death was to make the girls stop trying to escape. It's been a very difficult few days because I was reliving the whole nightmare I had already been through with your older brother. Anyway, the long and short of it is, the girls were rescued, and Mary's body is being returned tomorrow, where we will bury her ourselves."

The brothers looked stricken at the news of what happened to Nurse.

That made Lorelei feel better. Although Nurse was set in her ways and potentially a pain in the butt to a lot of people, Lorelei hadn't had any problem with her. But Mary had raised all of Gerard's children over many years—and even Gerard too as a child—so the family ties were strong. Gerard's sons were still in a daze as they listened.

Joe, Gerard's brother, then spoke. "I don't understand why you didn't tell us about their safe return. You know we would have been there to help and to support you after what you've already been through."

"They've barely been home for one day. Plus I've been sorting out who is behind all this. And fast, before the company was impacted."

"Of course. Always the company. Jesus, even when it was your own daughter," Joe said, shaking his head.

One of Gerard's sons nodded. "But it would have been devastating to the company shares and would have been a sign of weakness," he said. "Lots of our business competitors would have taken the chance to completely annihilate us, if they could have."

"Exactly," Gerard said, sounding surprised at his son's insights.

Lorelei glanced at Griffin and whispered, "Feels weird to be here for a family meeting right now."

"Maybe," he said, "but that's where we need to be with all the players in one room."

Just then Gerard's wife walked in, yawning, tying her robe around her. "Good Lord, I only got in during the wee hours of the morning and look at what's going on here."

"*What's going on?*" Gerard asked, his voice full of contempt.

As soon as she had entered, several security men stepped up, blocking her escape.

"What's going on is that the jig is up for you."

She looked at him in surprise. "What are you talking about?"

Although they suspected Wendy was responsible, they hadn't caught her in the act of doing anything involved with this mess.

Amelia Rose brought it all to a head. She walked over, stood in front of her mother, and said, "Did you really get me kidnapped in Thailand and have Nurse killed?"

Her mother stared at her in horror. "What are you talking about? Of course not. I would never do that!"

"Actually you would," Gerard said. "Particularly after I said no way were you getting custody of Amelia Rose."

At that, his wife turned her fury against him. "She's my daughter."

"She's also my daughter," Gerard said, fatigue in his voice. "I was more than happy to share custody. Until you pulled this stunt."

"I didn't do anything," she snapped. "How can you even begin to think I'd hurt Amelia Rose?"

But then Lorelei understood something else. "I just heard your voice in the stables," she said. "You did something to disguise it, but I figured it out."

Wendy turned to her and, in a mocking and disdainful way, said, "You're already traumatized from being kidnapped, and now you're pointing blame at me and expect anybody in their right minds to believe you? Obviously you need some time off." She turned to her husband. "I suggest we lay her off and give her a paid holiday. I'm sure we can find somebody better suited to teach Amelia Rose whatever it is you think she needs from a private tutor," she continued with a roll of her eyes. "But we certainly don't want somebody who is as mentally unbalanced as Lorelei is now."

"Well, if I am mentally unbalanced," Lorelei said in a calm voice, "I know who to blame."

"And who's that?" Wendy asked, calling her bluff.

"You," Lorelei said, turning to Amelia Rose. "It'll be okay, sweetie." Lorelei took that moment to have Amelia Rose taken from the room by her two security guards.

Lorelei continued, "You wouldn't necessarily hurt Amelia Rose, not physically at least, but you would consider these three kidnappings as, to you, a *small* emotional pain for her to endure if you end up with the twenty-five-million-dollar ransom. Wasn't that the amount Gerard was to pay? It's an interesting figure, but I'm sure, if we worked out what you thought these twelve years with Gerard were worth, you'd probably come up with something like that. And, of course, you had to pay for the men who you hired to do this, both here locally and in Thailand. But the clincher was hearing you in the stables, now that I think about it. I should have recognized your voice right off the bat because even the men who rescued us asked some questions that I didn't put together. Until now."

"What are you talking about?" Wendy asked as she huffed and walked to one of the chairs and threw herself elegantly across the upholstery.

Lorelei had never really understood how women could make simple movements just like that so smooth. Lorelei would look like a galloping horse if she tried to pull off something like that, but, then again, Wendy had good looks and Gerard's money and coaches for every conceivable thing that she could possibly want. So maybe Wendy had a coach for learning how to show disdain with a physical movement.

"You're the only one who would want Nurse killed," Lorelei said. "Nurse hated you, and you hated Nurse."

"Well, I certainly didn't hate her enough to have her murdered," she said in disbelief. "Oh, my Lord, you certainly need a holiday, if that's where your mind is at," she said.

Good God, trouble was, Wendy made everything sound so sensible, that this was all Lorelei's ludicrous beliefs. Lorelei wasn't even sure how to get through to Wendy. Lorelei looked to Griffin with a question in her eyes.

"The thing is, you are the only one who *would* want to kill Mary," Gerard said slowly. "You have always wanted me to get rid of her. You wanted me to buy her a little cottage somewhere and kick her away, even though the only family she had was us."

"She doesn't *have* you," Wendy said. "Good God, she's the hired help. It's not like they are blood. They are servants. They don't mean anything." She looked at Lorelei with a wave of her hand, and she laughed. "You didn't really think you would be wife number two, did you?"

"Oh, you mean, wife number four? Because you're number three, of course. No, I certainly have no intention of becoming wife number four. Gerard and I are definitely not suited. But then neither are you two. Nurse wanted Gerard to get rid of you, though didn't she? Especially lately?" She watched Wendy's face pinch tighter.

Gerard groaned. "Can we stick to the issue at hand?"

"The issue at hand are these preposterous accusations," Wendy said. She got to her feet, another purely elegant movement that had Lorelei wondering how she managed to pull it off. "I need sleep, so I'm going back to bed. Whenever you guys sort this out, you can let me know."

"Not quite," Lorelei said calmly.

When the guards assigned to Wendy boxed her in, she frowned and stepped back.

Lorelei turned toward Griffin and asked him, "Griffin, you have anything to add?"

Griffin smiled and said, "I'd like to know where you were, Wendy, when everybody was in Thailand."

"Well, I certainly don't have to answer your questions," Wendy said. "Good God, Gerard, are you really suggesting that I had something to do with my own daughter's kidnapping? That I would put her through something like that?" She shook her head. "That's low, even for you."

GRIFFIN WATCHED WENDY'S body language, something to reveal who her partner was in this. He already knew she was guilty, but it was a matter of finding who else was guilty with her. She continued to con the crowd, to spread her disdain around the room, her gaze mocking as she glanced at every person, landing on Lorelei at her side, the corner of her mouth turning down with an extra shot of venom for her. But when she looked at Gerard's brother, her gaze slid right by.

And Griffin knew.

"Of course she didn't do it alone," Griffin said. "She couldn't have planned this herself. Not enough smarts. So it's really all about who would partner with you to make sure that you were both looked after in the future. Knowing that, at some point in time, Gerard would retire and would hand over control of his company to his sons, you needed someone who would gain power from this kidnapping plan in addition to you. Or at least to make your partner in crime think he was getting an equal deal. But you didn't have the connections to set up a long-distance kidnapping in Thailand."

"Of course I didn't," she said. "And who are you?"

He waved his hand, as if telling her that her question wasn't important or that she wasn't important. He had no intention of answering her. "So I guess the real question is, what agreement did you make? And the first one to volunteer information and to help out, of course, will get a better deal."

She stared at him in mockery. "Does that work for you often?"

"Oh, it works a whole lot more often than you would think. We can already prove your involvement. You're the one who set up the trip to Thailand, the planning—like for hotel rooms and no security, and made sure that Nurse went, even though Nurse didn't want to go," he said smoothly. "The question is, who found and paid for the local men in Thailand? What about the extra men here?" He remembered the man barking orders at the hotel, where the three females had originally stayed. "I mean, we found several of your cohorts in the barn, of course, but where else would you find men for hire if you wanted a good ride?" He deliberately left the innuendo hanging.

She glared at him and said, "I do believe you're insulting me."

He shook his head immediately. "Good God, no. I couldn't be bothered. There's a time and a place for everything, and I've already figured out who your partner is. So the question is, will you give us the information first or will he?"

"Who is it?" Gerard demanded.

"Oh, no," Griffin said. "She gets one last chance right now. Otherwise MI6 gets her."

"That'll never happen," she said, but her demeanor stiffened as if suddenly worried.

"Well, the problem is, the other person involved has no intention of going down alone and taking the fall for you as the mastermind behind it all. The sentence will be quite a bit stiffer for you, Wendy."

"How does that work?" she asked on a disbelieving

laugh. "It should be easier. It's not like I did anything."

"Right," he said, seeing the first cracks in her facade.

Gerard, staring at his wife in horror, said, "Dear God, you *did* do this." He looked at Griffin. "And who else? I'll fucking kill him."

"Sadly"—Griffin looked at Gerard—"your brother."

On those words, his brother bolted from the office, past the two guards, racing for the front door. He came head-to-head with Jax. And it was all over, just like that.

When Jax pushed Joe back into the office, Wendy stared at him with hatred in her eyes. "All you had to do was sit there and completely deny everything, but, no, that was well beyond you, wasn't it?"

He glared at her. "What kind of a fucking mother would do that to her daughter? And to hate the child's nurse so much that you arranged for her to be killed as a lesson? God, poor Mary. She was my nurse growing up too. But, no, you were adamant on that score." He shook his head. "You're just scum."

"And what are you?" Lorelei asked in shock. "Except the scum's lover?"

Joe stared at her in horror. "You've got to be kidding. I wouldn't touch that well-used body for the life of me."

At that, Wendy screamed in outrage.

But Gerard's roar silenced everyone. He stood and stared at his brother. "After all I've been through, you would do this to me?"

Joe sneered at him. "Even back then, you were father's favorite. You were the poor son who'd been kidnapped, your own son murdered. It's the only reason he gave you the lion's share of the company. He felt sorry for you. He wanted to stop his own guilt for not keeping you safe."

"No," Gerard roared. "He felt guilty, sure, but nothing like I felt. He didn't *give* me the company. I earned it. As I've grown the family business one thousand times over since then, his trust in me has been proven. You were nothing but a wastrel, playing your days away, so damn sure you would get half, and yet, do nothing for it."

"Like hell." Joe shook his head, his face twisted with anger and jealousy. "He never loved me like he loved you. And you were so set on giving your daughter control of the company, over me, who's been working there as long as you have, Gerard? Really? I wanted Amelia Rose to die for many reasons, but especially so you had to deal with that same loss all over again.

"It's only one-quarter of the pain I went through every damn day listening to Father spout off how you were just like him. A businessman through and through, and why couldn't I be more like him and *you*." He spat that last word, making it obvious that was the last thing Joe wanted to be. "And you so generously let me keep my shares and work in the company, keeping a paycheck rolling through so I could support my family, while you rake in millions a year all for yourself."

"Millions I *earn*." Gerard stared at his brother in disgust, but there was no surprise in his expression. "You should be thankful I'm such a family man. I should have cut you loose when I first took over the company for Father. You've always been lazy. A self-centered entitled bastard." He looked at his wife in disgust. "It makes sense now. Joe has been dealing with a lot of Asian companies recently. That's how he found the people to do your dirty work in Thailand. And was he to get half the ransom money?"

The look on her face made him laugh. "Of course not,"

Gerard said, shaking his head, still chuckling. "You weren't giving any of the ransom money to him, were you? So the company went to Joe? But you still didn't have the majority ownership, even pooling Amelia Rose's shares with Joe's. At my death, my sons own fifty percent of the company, with Joe and Amelia Rose owning the other fifty percent. It's still half for the boys and half for Joe and my daughter. No one completely owns the company. Forcing them to work together, which was my plan. But which wouldn't happen until I died. Hell, even with me dead, this wouldn't make Joe happy. Joe doesn't have the ability to be happy." He snorted. "Neither do you, Wendy."

She shrugged. "Causing you pain was a lot of it on my part. Joe wanted you and Amelia Rose dead, but I didn't want my daughter involved any more than she was. So the plan was for me to disappear with her, and then you'd have an accident, Gerard. Maybe your sons too." She glanced at Gerard and Joe, staring at her like she was a nasty virus that might spread. "Not like Joe cares about them either."

Gerard sank back into his big leather chair, the huge man diminished by the family of blackhearts plotting against him.

The room was suddenly filled with MI6 men, as all their prisoners were led away.

CHAPTER 14

LORELEI STARED AT the suddenly silent and almost empty room and gave a broken laugh. "There's nothing, really, to laugh at. But it's either that or cry. This is just too unbelievable."

Griffin wrapped an arm around her, pulled her close, and said, "But now it's over. We have a team picking up the hired men in Thailand."

She buried her head against his chest and whispered, "Thank God for that." As she turned to look around, Amelia Rose was in her father's arms, her arms tight around him too. And Lorelei knew that, although this was one of those life lessons that was almost impossible to forget, Amelia Rose would be fine—eventually. Lorelei wasn't sure how fine she would be though. Amelia Rose would have everything money could buy to help her over this. But she also had the one thing that money couldn't buy which would get her over this the best and which would help her the most.

Her father's love.

It was a good ninety minutes later when Lorelei headed to bed. She was exhausted. Her mind still buzzed with everything that had happened. She'd been separated somewhere along the line from Griffin, so that their statements could be taken by MI6. Now things were getting back to normal. All the MI6 agents had been given rooms to accommodate their stay as they continued their investigation later today, after getting some sleep first. Lorelei suddenly found herself outside Griffin's bedroom. She snorted at that but had no problem walking inside and crashing on his bed. As far as she was concerned, that was the best idea she'd had in a long time. She was just drifting off when the door opened. She smiled and muttered, "Where'd you think I'd be?"

He quickly shucked his clothes and crawled in beside her. He pulled her up close, and she said, "Finally."

"Sleep," he said. "We'll talk in the morning."

"It is morning," she muttered, yet sleep reached up to claim her. The last thing she heard was, "Okay, later this morning." And she drifted off.

When she awoke, she felt a furnace beside her. She rolled into it, welcoming its heat as it chased away the chill in her soul. It was beyond comprehension that Amelia Rose's mother had been behind all of that terror and had used the opportunity to get rid of Nurse at the same time. What was wrong with people who thought murder was considered a reasonable action to take? And, of course, Joe and Wendy hadn't picked up the money because they were well aware it had been a trick and a trap. Lorelei wondered what would have happened if they'd gotten away with kidnapping them the second or third time.

Would there have been yet another ransom, or would that be a case of just *kill them off and who cared?*

She was still so damn tired. She didn't want to move, and she had no idea what would happen in terms of her and Griffin. Obviously he would leave, and she had to rethink what she wanted to do with her life, not to mention about Amelia Rose. Was it time for her to go to school and to meet other friends and not have a private tutor? Probably. She'd grown up a lot over this. Lorelei was good at what she did, and what Amelia Rose really needed to heal now was time with her father.

Lorelei hoped that these horrid circumstances had brought some good to Amelia Rose and her father too—a closeness, a new beginning, a more transparent sense of communication—not to mention to Gerard's sons too. She was glad that they weren't involved. It would be good if Gerard could ease up some of the control that he held over them and over the company, could give them bigger roles, could make them feel like they had a bigger part in the company. Even though both sons worked for the company, they were not high enough in the company to have any actual power.

"What are you thinking?" Griffin murmured.

"I'm wondering about the future," she said honestly. "My job, your job, and Gerard. I'll have to deal with the family dynamics."

"Do you think they'll be okay?" he asked.

"Yes," she said. "And obviously way better off than with a woman who was prepared to do something like that to the family for money."

"Do you think it was for money or to keep custody?"

"With her, maybe I should have said for *power*," she explained, "because I don't think love was the determining factor in this case. As long as she had control over her daughter, she still had access to a lot of money. And how sad is that?"

"Very," he said, nuzzling her neck. "You should be sleeping and not worrying about other people's family problems."

"I know, but while I've been here, I felt like I was part of the family. And now? Now I think it's time for a change, but it might be too soon for Amelia Rose."

"I'm sure it is. She's already lost Nurse and now her mom, at least in any way that counts."

"Right," Lorelei said. "How do you deal with that kind of betrayal?"

"Slowly and one bite at a time," he said. "And with Gerard always around to help her."

"Yes," she said. "I think that's the most important recovery piece that he needs to understand, how his presence is so necessary to her healing."

"She might need you too."

"I think for a little while, yes," she said. "For a transition period but not forever. She's certainly grown up a lot. I mean she's eleven going on twenty-one."

He chuckled at that. "She's a very precocious child. I alternate from calling her woman to child to something in between."

"Because she is, and she's still in that young version of whatever we should call it."

"That preteen. *Precocious* preteen."

She chuckled. "Yeah, exactly."

"And what do you want to do?" he asked. "You've been looking after other people's kid for a long time."

"Well, not in the capacity you mean. I'm a tutor, but I don't know if I want to do that anymore. You learn a lot when your future is suddenly taken away from you. Now that I have one again, I need to rethink things."

"It does happen that way, indeed. You have to put a priority on some things, prioritize your life," he said. "And that can be hard."

"It can be deadly," she said. "I really don't know."

"Well, don't rush into anything," he said. "You have time."

She smiled. "I do now, thanks to you. Do you think they would have killed us?"

"I don't know," he said. "Depending on the brother's level of involvement, it was to his benefit to ensure that Amelia Rose not survive. But I don't know how the mother who would have handled that. Possibly an unfortunate accident down the road. As for you, they couldn't let you live to talk."

"Nice. *Not.* I guess it depended on the money, didn't it?" she said caustically. "Something I'll have a hard time with."

"Sure, just understand that Amelia Rose is young and strong, and she will recover, and this is a terrible family scenario, but it's not *your* family scenario."

"I know," she said. She smiled up into his eyes and said, "What about you?"

"What about me?" he asked, and then he yawned.

She gently rubbed his unshaven cheek and asked, "When are you leaving?"

He winced. "Probably soon. I don't really know."

"Sounds like we both have things to think about," she said.

He nodded. "We do, but just think. We're in control. We can choose what we want to do right now."

"I know what I want to do right now," she said. "The question is, what do we want to do after *right now?*" And she reached up and kissed him gently.

"Well, I like to work on one thing at a time," he said smoothly. "So how about we focus on that *right now* thing, and then we'll worry about the rest?"

She chuckled. "So, in other words, make no plans right now?"

"I know one thing," he said. "I don't want to lose contact with you."

She smiled, nodded, and said, "Agreed. In that case, as long as we do our best to find a way to make something work, then nothing else really matters, does it?"

He smiled and said, "Well, some things matter." And he nudged his hips against her.

She felt the heat and the hard ridge against her smooth skin.

"You're wearing too many clothes," he whispered.

She chuckled. "I'm sure a handy guy like you can take care of that." And, within seconds, she was flipped onto her back, and her nightdress was up and over her head. Laughter, bright and joyous, peeled out as she wrapped her arms around him. "You're such a can-do type of guy. Why don't you show me what you can do?"

"You mean, show you more?" he asked. "I already rescued you twice, by the way."

She placed a finger against his lips, stopping the flow of words, and said, "How about, instead of talking, you just show me?"

He lowered his head, and he kissed her gently several times, and then finally he deepened the kiss until she moaned with joy.

She wrapped her arms snugly around his neck and said, "Not too bad a start. I can't wait to see how you finish."

He chuckled and proceeded to show her with his hands, lips, and tongue, stroking, learning as she moaned and twisted beneath him. Every movement that brought her pleasure, every movement that caused her to still in surprise, only to arch up in need.

She cried out time and time again until finally she demanded, "Enough teasing. I want you now." She hooked her legs around him as he settled between them. She looped her arms around his neck, tugging him close, and whispered, "Kiss me like you mean it."

He stopped, looked at her. "Every kiss I've given you is because I mean it. This isn't a dalliance," he whispered gently, caressing her cheek with his lips, his tongue sliding along the edge of her lower lip and then inside to war with hers. He pulled back ever-so-slightly. "This is for us. Not just for today, not just for tomorrow, but for as long as we want it."

She smiled, wrapping her legs tighter around his hips and whispered, "Then how about forever?"

And he plunged deep, taking her all the way home.

EPILOGUE

J AX HAD SEEN it coming, but he wondered how they would make it work. As far as he understood, Kerrick and Amanda were doing just fine in Paris. But Lorelei and Griffin? … Well, they had hit it off right from the beginning. But Jax couldn't be happier for his friend. It was a lonely lifestyle these SEALs had chosen to lead, and each and every one of them had come to this point as a jumping off spot to something different, to making a choice to do something else.

He hadn't told Griffin but Jax's agreement to come on this mission was so that he could take the lead on one op and one op only. He was leaving the military, and he was leaving everything to do with this type of life. The Mavericks team had asked Jax specifically to help Griffin as a warm-up to doing his one mission sometime later. He figured that it was the same for Kerrick and for Griffin. Jax wasn't sure about joining the Mavericks unit for what would be his one big job, but the unit trained everybody before they took the lead on their one mission and then were done. But, as Jax thought about it, nobody in the Mavericks unit needed training.

This was like the peak of their careers for them. Jax didn't know if they would all be brought back to do something else. It was possible though, and Jax would consider it.

He also knew that most of them were getting paid enough money that they wouldn't have to work again. He'd never discussed that part either with Griffin or Kerrick. Jax didn't even know if Griffin knew what Kerrick had gone through. What Jax did know was that the next job was his to head up. He hoped that he had a couple weeks or a month or two before then. Hell, he'd be happy to have a year or two in between these particular jobs.

They were hard and intense, but, once done, then the op was done, and so was he. He didn't have friends or family to worry about, so he was in a much easier situation than Griffin and Kerrick. Although, now that they had met and been partnered up for these Mavericks operations, things had changed for those guys too. That didn't mean that they, in any way, shape, or form, were ready to go out the same as Jax was. They'd all come to the point where, if this was the last mission for them, then that was the last mission, and they didn't really care to go on any more missions.

Neither did he. He was moving on to something different. He just didn't know what. He had a hankering for travel, to see the world as a tourist for a change, instead of skulking through the night in the shadows of darkness, watching other shadows move as they tried to take over worlds and governments and individuals.

Sitting on a beach and watching the sunrise would be a pretty decent way to spend his time, and sitting on the same damn beach and watching each new sunset would be a unique opportunity for him to just relax, maybe with a cold beer and with a friend or two. Now that would make his life pretty damn perfect.

He was headed back home again. He had been on his phone, setting up arrangements for his apartment and making sure his landlady knew he would arrive soon. The silly things in life that you had to organize. As he landed back in California and grabbed his single bag and headed outside the airport, his cell buzzed.

He glanced down at the screen, groaned, and said, "Hell no. What?"

"How tired out are you?"

"Fucking tired," he said. "It's not like I got much sleep on the last job."

"That was two days ago," the man said in exasperation.

Jax heard something in that voice, and he said, "Hell, Griffin, is that you?"

Griffin chuckled. "Hell yeah, it's me. Is that okay?"

"I don't know," Jax said. "What do you want?"

Immediately all the humor fled as Griffin said, "We need you."

"Are you coming with me?"

"No. Somebody will though."

"Why is it always like that?" he asked. "Some of these jobs are getting pretty thin for just one or two of us."

"If it can be more, it'll be more. I promise I won't send you out without backup."

He snorted at that. "But it won't be you though, right? You'll be holed up somewhere nice and cozy with Lorelei."

"If I could join you, I would," Griffin said regretfully. "Lorelei and I will see each other on a regular basis now, spending time with Amelia Rose too. We're giving the child time to adapt before Lorelei leaves."

"I'm almost jealous," Jax said. "*Almost* but not quite."

Griffin snorted. "Your time will come. You won't even see it happening, and, before you know it, it'll be right there in your face."

"I doubt it," he said, "but whatever. So, what's the job?"

Griffin took a long, slow breath and said, "You won't like it."

"I never liked any of 'em," he said. "So what's the deal?"

"We've got a cruise ship that's been taken over."

"Pirates? I'm one man. Remember that?"

"It's a one-man job. We need somebody who can go in and take them out, one by one."

"I still am not going alone. Someone has to watch my back."

"Do you remember Beau?"

"Hell yeah, I remember Beau. That man could eat crawfish like nobody else I've ever seen," Jax said. "Then again he's huge. He can't hide anywhere. He's too damn big."

"Well, he won't be eating crawfish this time. And he won't need to hide. As a matter of fact, he'll be shooting bullets at pirates. He always was a dang good sharpshooter. So he'll meet you there."

"Meet me where?"

Griffin snorted. "Off the Florida coast. You should be there right on time."

"No," Jax said. "I just got off the goddamn plane in California."

"So you're already packed, right? You hear your name on the PA system? Yeah, that's to go pick up your tickets. You're flying out now."

And, with that, Griffin hung up.

Jax swore.

This concludes Book 2 of The Mavericks: Griffin.

Read about Jax: The Mavericks, Book 3

The Mavericks: Jax (Book #3)

What happens when the very men—trained to make the hard decisions—come up against the rules and regulations that hold them back from doing what needs to be done? They either stay and work within the constraints given to them or they walk away. Only now, for a select few, they have another option:

The Mavericks. A covert black ops team that steps up and break all the rules … but gets the job done.

Welcome to a new military romance series by *USA Today* best-selling author Dale Mayer. A series where you meet new friends in this raw and compelling look at the men who keep us safe every day from the darkness where they operate—and live—in the shadows … until someone special helps them step into the light.

No time to rest. The world is a mess …

He'd barely made it home from helping Griffin only to find himself called to rescue a doctor on a cruise ship overtaken by pirates in their search for Abigail Dalton. The pirates had no trouble killing passengers until they found the right woman. With one man at his side, Jax sneaks onto the ship to rescue her.

When she heard the gunfire, Abby hid in the venting on the ship. When a man susses out her hiding place, she's sure her world is about to end. Only Jax is on her side; yet he came with just one man to help. Stunned, she stays close as

Jax frees the ship and keeps her safe—until they find out the real reason for this nightmare, when she's forced to England to face the two-legged monster of her nightmares …

The safest place is at Jax's side, but Abby knows all too well how slippery this monster really is and how easily he steps from the shadows to grab his victims …

Find book 3 here!
To find out more visit Dale Mayer's website.
https://geni.us/DMJaxUniversal

Author's Note

Thank you for reading Griffin: The Mavericks, Book 2! If you enjoyed the book, please take a moment and leave a short review.

Dear reader,

I love to hear from readers, and you can contact me at my website: www.dalemayer.com or at my Facebook author page. To be informed of new releases and special offers, sign up for my newsletter or follow me on BookBub. And if you are interested in joining Dale Mayer's Reader Group, here is the Facebook sign up page.
http://geni.us/DaleMayerFBGroup

Cheers,
Dale Mayer

About the Author

Dale Mayer is a *USA Today* best-selling author, best known for her SEALs military romances, her Psychic Visions series, and her Lovely Lethal Garden cozy series. Her contemporary romances are raw and full of passion and emotion (Broken But … Mending, Hathaway House series). Her thrillers will keep you guessing (Kate Morgan, By Death series), and her romantic comedies will keep you giggling (*It's a Dog's Life*, a stand-alone novella; and the Broken Protocols series, starring Charming Marvin, the cat).

Dale honors the stories that come to her—and some of them are crazy, break all the rules and cross multiple genres!

To go with her fiction, she also writes nonfiction in many different fields, with books available on résumé writing, companion gardening, and the US mortgage system. All her books are available in print and ebook format.

Connect with Dale Mayer Online

Dale's Website – www.dalemayer.com
Twitter – @DaleMayer
Facebook Page – geni.us/DaleMayerFBFanPage
Facebook Group – geni.us/DaleMayerFBGroup
BookBub – geni.us/DaleMayerBookbub
Instagram – geni.us/DaleMayerInstagram
Goodreads – geni.us/DaleMayerGoodreads
Newsletter – geni.us/DaleNews

Also by Dale Mayer

Published Adult Books:

Hathaway House

Aaron, Book 1

Brock, Book 2

Cole, Book 3

Denton, Book 4

Elliot, Book 5

Finn, Book 6

Gregory, Book 7

The K9 Files

Ethan, Book 1

Pierce, Book 2

Zane, Book 3

Blaze, Book 4

Lucas, Book 5

Parker, Book 6

Carter, Book 7

Lovely Lethal Gardens

Arsenic in the Azaleas, Book 1

Bones in the Begonias, Book 2

Corpse in the Carnations, Book 3

Daggers in the Dahlias, Book 4

Evidence in the Echinacea, Book 5

Footprints in the Ferns, Book 6

Gun in the Gardenias, Book 7

Handcuffs in the Heather, Book 8

Psychic Vision Series

Tuesday's Child

Hide 'n Go Seek

Maddy's Floor

Garden of Sorrow

Knock Knock…

Rare Find

Eyes to the Soul

Now You See Her

Shattered

Into the Abyss

Seeds of Malice

Eye of the Falcon

Itsy-Bitsy Spider

Unmasked

Deep Beneath

From the Ashes

Psychic Visions Books 1–3

Psychic Visions Books 4–6

Psychic Visions Books 7–9

By Death Series

Touched by Death

Haunted by Death

Chilled by Death

By Death Books 1–3

Broken Protocols – Romantic Comedy Series

Cat's Meow

Cat's Pajamas

Cat's Cradle
Cat's Claus
Broken Protocols 1-4

Broken and... Mending
Skin
Scars
Scales (of Justice)
Broken but... Mending 1-3

Glory
Genesis
Tori
Celeste
Glory Trilogy

Biker Blues
Morgan: Biker Blues, Volume 1
Cash: Biker Blues, Volume 2

SEALs of Honor
Mason: SEALs of Honor, Book 1
Hawk: SEALs of Honor, Book 2
Dane: SEALs of Honor, Book 3
Swede: SEALs of Honor, Book 4
Shadow: SEALs of Honor, Book 5
Cooper: SEALs of Honor, Book 6
Markus: SEALs of Honor, Book 7
Evan: SEALs of Honor, Book 8
Mason's Wish: SEALs of Honor, Book 9
Chase: SEALs of Honor, Book 10
Brett: SEALs of Honor, Book 11
Devlin: SEALs of Honor, Book 12

Heroes for Hire

Liam's Lily: Heroes for Hire, Book 14
North's Nikki: Heroes for Hire, Book 15
Anders's Angel: Heroes for Hire, Book 16
Reyes's Raina: Heroes for Hire, Book 17
Dezi's Diamond: Heroes for Hire, Book 18
Vince's Vixen: Heroes for Hire, Book 19
Ice's Icing: Heroes for Hire, Book 20
Heroes for Hire, Books 1–3
Heroes for Hire, Books 4–6
Heroes for Hire, Books 7–9
Heroes for Hire, Books 10–12
Heroes for Hire, Books 13–15

SEALs of Steel

Badger: SEALs of Steel, Book 1
Erick: SEALs of Steel, Book 2
Cade: SEALs of Steel, Book 3
Talon: SEALs of Steel, Book 4
Laszlo: SEALs of Steel, Book 5
Geir: SEALs of Steel, Book 6
Jager: SEALs of Steel, Book 7
The Final Reveal: SEALs of Steel, Book 8
SEALs of Steel, Books 1–4
SEALs of Steel, Books 5–8
SEALs of Steel, Books 1–8

The Mavericks

Kerrick, Book 1
Griffin, Book 2
Jax, Book 3
Beau, Book 4
Asher, Book 5
Ryker, Book 6

Miles, Book 7

Nico, Book 8

Keane, Book 9

Lennox, Book 10

Gavin, Book 11

Shane, Book 12

Collections

Dare to Be You…

Dare to Love…

Dare to be Strong…

RomanceX3

Standalone Novellas

It's a Dog's Life

Riana's Revenge

Second Chances

Published Young Adult Books:

Family Blood Ties Series

Vampire in Denial

Vampire in Distress

Vampire in Design

Vampire in Deceit

Vampire in Defiance

Vampire in Conflict

Vampire in Chaos

Vampire in Crisis

Vampire in Control

Vampire in Charge

Family Blood Ties Set 1–3

Family Blood Ties Set 1–5

Family Blood Ties Set 4–6

Family Blood Ties Set 7–9

Sian's Solution, A Family Blood Ties Series Prequel
    Novelette

Design series

Dangerous Designs

Deadly Designs

Darkest Designs

Design Series Trilogy

Standalone

In Cassie's Corner

Gem Stone (a Gemma Stone Mystery)

Time Thieves

Published Non-Fiction Books:

Career Essentials

Career Essentials: The Résumé

Career Essentials: The Cover Letter

Career Essentials: The Interview

Career Essentials: 3 in 1